SCOTTISH LOVE STORIES

SCOTTISH LOVE STORIES

SELECTED BY SUSIE MAGUIRE
AND MARION SINCLAIR

POLYGON
EDINBURGH

© Editorial arrangements Polygon 1995

(pages 208-210 constitute an extension of the copyright page)

First published in 1995 by
Polygon
22 George Square
Edinburgh
EH8 9LF

Reprinted in 1996

Set in Weiss by WestKey Ltd, Falmouth, Cornwall
Printed and bound in Great Britain by Short Run Press, Exeter

A CIP Record for this title is available.

The Publisher acknowledges subsidy from

THE SCOTTISH ARTS COUNCIL

towards the publication of this volume.

CONTENTS

The Lass o' Patie's Mill

The lass o' Patie's mill,
  So bonny, blythe, and gay,
In spite of all my skill,
  Hath stole my heart away.
When tedding of the hay,
  Bare-headed on the green,
Love 'midst her locks did play,
  And wanton'd in her een.

Her arms, white, round, and smooth,
  Breasts rising in their dawn,
To age it would give youth,
  To press them with his hand.
Thro' all my spirits ran
  An extasy of bliss,
When I such sweetness fan'd
  Wrapt in a balmy kiss.

Without the help of art,
  Like flowers which grace the wild,
She did her sweets impart,
  Whene'er she spoke or smil'd.
Her looks they were so mild,
  Free from affected pride,
She me to love beguil'd;
  I wish'd her for my bride.

O had I all the wealth
  Hopetoun's high mountains fill,
Insur'd lang life and health,
  And pleasure at my will;
I'd promise and fulfil,
  That none but bonny she,
The lass o' Patie's mill,
  Shou'd share the same with me.

ALLAN RAMSAY
1686–1758

PREFACE

My authority for undertaking this introduction is a) being asked to b) being Scottish c) reading a lot d) writing stories and e) having loved, or at least suffered from inflammation and fracture of the heart. Perhaps those are credential enough. Raymond Carver says something about there being no seniority in writing, in which case any writer's love story is as good as the love s/he holds in readiness to give. And anyone who can wield a keyboard can write about love, can't they? Anyone can dream. . . .

When Madame X slips into the bed-chamber of Monsieur Y at Chateau Z, when she drops her corset onto the Louis Quinze and they slither between satin sheets, we know we're on familiar territory. When eyes smoulder and bosoms heave; when candles flicker and breath comes in gasps, we can just picture the Romantic Novelist swathed in pink, on her chaise longue, popping vitamins and petting her lap dog as she dictates, while across the room a young woman attired in top-to-toe Laura Ashley taps it out on the word-processor. Ah, Romance! Ah, Tradition!

But beneath her Alice band, behind her desk, does Ms Prim dream of Brad Pitt or Kirsty Wark? Is she content to dream? Does she strap into leather and cruise when her day's work is done? Or does she go home to baked beans on toast and the *People's Friend*, and sing 'Ooh Baby, Yeah' to her budgie?

Pardon me for asking the obvious, but What Is Love? Supposedly an emotional boomerang. The word itself is confusing. LOVE, hmm, ponder. Flirtation, frustration, fornication, more specific and less love-ly words, often under-used when we talk about our relationships. 'I fell into copulation'—has a wee ring to it, doesn't it?

Talking about love doesn't make it any better than it is— remember *Dynasty*, in which the characters simultaneously proclaimed love and each others' names, in case there should be some confusion of identity; how they employed the term 'I love you' as bindingly as an oil-lease contract?

And what is Scottish love? Roamin' in the gloamin'? Irn Bru and wet midgey evenings in Fort William? Necking in North Berwick? Is that love? In popular culture, love has been everything from the delicate language of the flowers to songs full of graphic descriptions of the sexual act. So how do we know it when we find it? How do we know when it's gone? Is it genetic, is it in the collective unconscious? Is it worn beneath the kilt?

Perhaps love only truly dwells in the imagination, to which the next best thing is the printed page. Enter the fiction writer, spreading out that tray of marvels beyond our grasp, or horrors from which we shield our eyes (or more probably at which we keek through our fingers).

In this collection there should be food for the soul of the cynic and the afflicted alike. Keep the Kleenex handy but equally beware choking to death over your butter mints from hysterical laughter. As they say, if you can't laugh at life, you're either dead or in love. (Actually, I just made that up.)

No longer being in love is an underwritten situation. Like Delia Smith and her limes, I urge you to consider the 'downer' love story as a wonderful thing. There are times when a tale of rage and frustration at desertion and adultery can warm the cockles of your heart. Better still a collection of such tales, as a morale-boosting gift for the recently rejected. A bulging volume, written from the broken hearts and manic minds of the jilted and the spurned, just to even the balance against all those glossy tales of happiness. What's wrong with looking at the Dark Side? There's some of that here too. Ooh baby, yeah.

You don't have to be 'in love' to read this book. It's low on mush. None of the authors possesses a pink fluffy negligée and bobbly mules to wear while dictating, or if they do they haven't declared it in these pages. They have created love stories whilst fingering small grubby pencils, or fondling their fonts. Remember that, and enjoy.

Susie Maguire

Ian Hamilton Finlay

A BROKEN
ENGAGEMENT

When I was young and we had our money—we lost it afterwards—we kept a maid. That is, we kept several one after another, but I remember only one of them, the maid Peggy, a plump, grown-up girl with rowan-berry-red cheeks, black hair, a white apron, and a black dress . . .

Our house was two-storied, and Peggy must have had a bedroom in it, but the kitchen was really more her place. I mean 'her place' in the nice sense: the place you would normally go to look for her, and where, in the evening when the work was finished, she was free to amuse herself just as I was in the drawing-room, upstairs. The kitchen was downstairs, in the basement. This was just under ground level and was reached by a flight of old-fashioned, steep stone stairs which were lit by a gas-lamp even by day.

I used to go down there a lot in the evening, after tea. At that hour, with the several straight-backed chairs tidied, the table newly scrubbed, and the day's dishes and pots and pans washed and laid by, there was a feeling in there like that of a sunset—a beautiful, still, sad sunset when the birch and pine trees, even the brackens, are so very, very still it is as if they have been bewitched . . . Just such a feeling was over the chairs, the dewy table, the neatly stacked dishes and the shining pots and pans that hung in a row from the same shelf.

'Peggy?' I would say as I came in. 'Peggy?—Peggy draw me a face.'

She might be seated in front of the big kitchen range which, being now closed and banked-up for the evening, was—in this indoor sunset—the equivalent of that faraway, bright rosy band above the woods. Or else she might be seated, hands propping her chin, at the table, bent over a love-story magazine, a weekly magazine printed on a coarse, off-white sort of paper and with illustrations in black line.

Almost certainly she would agree to draw me a face. And, in practice, that meant several faces, copied either from the illustrations to the love-stories in the magazine or from those to the advertisements (for corsets, cheap scent, and so on) that appeared on the pages towards the back. She would stand up, and crossing to the shelf beneath that for the dishes, she would fetch the writing-pad, the pencil and india rubber; then, having carefully sharpened the pencil to a fine point with the old kitchen-knife, she would begin to draw me a face . . .

How can I say how lovely it was? I would lean up close to her, my elbows on the table, scarcely breathing—breathing very slowly through my open mouth while I held my tongue curled up just as if there was some mysterious, radar connection between the carefulness of the moving pencil-point, and *its* . . . Then, after a while, a sort of painless pins-and-needles would start to creep up me, beginning, I think, in about the knees; and after another while I was half-asleep . . . As for the face Peggy drew, it was one with long, literally shiny eyelashes, two dots for nostrils, smiling rosebud lips, and bobbed hair. (This I pictured as being of a brown colour.) And, as soon as one face was completed, 'Now draw me another, Peggy,' I would say. Because I couldn't bear that she should stop drawing and so break the magical spell . . .

One night I met my mother at the head of the stairs down to the basement. She said, 'You're not to go down to see Peggy tonight.'

'Oh, but Mummy,' I protested, 'why can't I?'

'Never mind! Why should you, a child, be told why you can't? You just aren't to go down; that's all.'

I turned and went into the drawing-room, but later, my mother having for some reason gone up to her bedroom, I did go downstairs.

Everything in the sunset kitchen was just as usual, except that an unfamiliar, grown-up young man was seated on a kitchen chair, opposite Peggy, to one side of the range. He was seated very upright and very silent; and he wore a blue suit and had a red face and hands which, spread out stiffly on his blue knees, were exactly the colour of Lifebuoy soap. What was *he* doing here? I thought. And as he, it seemed to me, was ignoring Peggy, I decided to ignore him, too.

'Peggy?' I said. 'Peggy? Peggy, draw me a face.'

Imagine my astonishment when she shook her head and said, 'No. No faces tonight. Just you be a good little boy and run away back upstairs.'

And the young man, suddenly taking his eyes, as it were, from that rosy band above the woods, said, 'Go on, sonny. Listen. There's your Mummy calling you. Now run along.'

That, of course, was untrue, but I went. I left the two of them alone there, silent, their straight-backed chairs like two separate rocks. I wondered if they really were as bored as they seemed.

And after that the young man came into the kitchen in the evening quite often. Harry something was his name. Once he had a thick bandage across two fingers of his right hand. Peggy said he had hurt it at his work. He always sat very upright and very silent, and then he pretended to hear my mother calling on me from somewhere upstairs. One night when he wasn't there I noticed that Peggy was wearing a new ring . . .

'What's that?' I asked her.

I spoke softly, but even so I broke the magical spell that lay on us as we sat drawing faces out of the love-story magazine.

'That?' said Peggy. 'That's a ring.'

'Yes, I know,' I said. 'But what's it for, that ring?'

'It's an engagement ring,' she said.

'An engagement ring—what's that?'

'It means I'm going to be married.'

'Now?'

'Soon.'

'To Harry?'

'Yes, to Harry.'

'Oh. Now draw me another face. You've spoiled that face,' I said.

And the young man, Harry, came more, and then still more often. So that we never drew faces. I have the impression that he was in the kitchen—Peggy's kitchen—every night. And a long time, maybe four of five whole weeks, passed. The bad time had an end one night when, as I came into the kitchen expecting to see Harry there, I found Peggy all alone and, as I thought, fast asleep. Her arms were folded across the love-story magazine, which wasn't open, and her head was laid on her arms.

'Peggy? Peggy?' I said, shaking her by the shoulder. 'Peggy, draw me a face.'

After all, she wasn't asleep, but she didn't look up then—only shook her head once or twice.

'Oh go on,' I pleaded. 'Be a pal. Just one face.'

'No, please.' She shook her head again, several times. 'Please no faces tonight.'

'Oh *please*, Peggy. Please. Just one. If you do—,' I hesitated, '—if you do you'll be my best pal, for life.'

So Peggy stood up, and she went through the beautiful, still, sad sunset to fetch the drawing things from the shelf. Her eyes were swollen and red round the edges as though, maybe, she had been crying; and as she stood sharpening the pencil with the old kitchen knife I could see a red mark on her finger where she had had the ring. Then she opened the love-story magazine and began to draw me a face. I leaned up close to her, scarcely breathing; the painless pins-and-needles crept slowly up me. It was lovely! . . . Soon I was half-asleep. 🍂

Deirdre Chapman

THE NEW PLACE

Mrs Paton dabbled her toes in the Aegean and shivered.

The Aegean was tepid, like a big bath, she thought, run off a small immerser. Her shiver was spiritual. This same sea now fingering her ankles, titillating her bunion and shooting cool shafts of pleasure up the pain corridors from her boxy feet, this sea had carried fair Helen and Paris to Troy. Mighty Alexander had crossed it. Ulysses had ploughed his wild furrow through it. Poseidon ruled it.

'Home at last,' said Mrs Paton to herself and blushed.

She really was feeling most odd. The sun was nibbling at the nape of her neck, the rocks bit into her bottom, and the afternoon trembled about her in a way that was hard to contain. Down there her toes swam singly in the thick water, at once captured and liberated, like prawns in aspic.

Nothing moved but the sunlight on the surface of the bay, lumpy and metallic as crushed kitchen foil right out to the next brown island. Behind her the five concrete stories of the Poseidon Beach Hotel were screened by taller rocks. Stacked parallel and horizontal between their private baths and their sea views, Mr Paton on his twin bed, Bill and Mavis from Beckenham, Kent, Lee and Sharon from Boston, Mass., and the nice German couple snored off moussaka and Greek beer while their swimsuits baked dry for the evening dip. Unobserved, Mrs Paton launched herself into the water.

It came up only as far as her collar bone which, she thought, touching bottom, was just as well, for she had never learned to swim. She had felt no need standing every summer up to her pale calves in the North Sea, lusting after Europe on the other side.

But now as she spread her arms and trembled on her tiptoes, Earth, Air, Fire and Water competing for her, she awarded the golden apple to Water. 'I am in my element,' she said out loud, and laughed as she blushed.

Her large body floated free of gravity and ached with uplift like a pink satin gas-filled balloon. Her bosom spread itself splendidly beneath the surface, her cleavage a cushioned grotto for tired plankton. She moonwalked away from the rocks and music came on in her head, music for floating to shoeless, braless, corsetless. She recognized it as the lost music of the Greek world, the missing complement to the statues, the temples, the poetry. She tried to sing it in her mournful wobbly contralto but it eluded her.

A purple jellyfish sidled past, heading out to sea. A shoal of tiny nervous fish looked right, looked left, looked right again and streaked away in pursuit. High overhead a grey seabird circled.

Why, she thought, that's the first bird I've seen since I came to Greece.

She faced the sun and closed her eyes, and in the orange darkness thought of poor Leto, panting with second stage contractions, combing the Aegean for a place to give birth till Poseidon anchored Delos for her. She herself had had a half-hour journey to hospital on the back seat of a Mini, but there the comparison ended. Leto had produced Apollo and that was worth any amount of suffering, especially after the disappointment of a daughter, even Artemis.

Her own daughter had died within an hour of birth and after all these years the memory still held more guilt than sorrow. Ariadne, she had called her. The midwife had snorted with disapproval, afterwards adjusting her face mask in case a Presbyterian germ flew out and landed on the baby. But Ariadne had been beyond the niceties of sterility. Her husband had been shown in and said, 'Ariadne McFarlane Ross, then.' Mrs Paton always remembered that as her daughter's epitaph. They had trundled her back to the ward and, behind the chintz curtains they pulled to exclude grief, blood and private parts, she had wept. But even as she wept a subversive voice was whispering that the death of a weak female child was no tragedy. She should have had a son, a hero, but Mr Paton wasn't up to it.

Zeus had been shifty about his mistresses, a side of him she disapproved of though it was manifestly Greek. He had hidden Leto in the guise of a quail, and turned the passive Io into a cow. But jealous Hera had found and pursued them both, sending a gadfly to harry Io till she plunged into the sea. She herself would have shunned his cowskins and faced Hera woman to woman, not that she approved of easy virtue, but Hera reminded her of some of her more self-righteous friends, preaching at unmarried mothers under the cloak of welfare work and blaming the single woman in any triangle.

'Damn Hera,' she said. 'Damn them all.'

Up above the seabird rocked in a sudden puff of wind.

She remembered Silbury's Soups, but for whom she would not be here today, basking and bobbing and meditating. It was hard to feel anything warm and personal for such a large firm, but she owed it to them to try. It was their kindness, together with two packets of their Scotch Broth, two Minestrone, one Spring Vegetable and one Lentil with Ham, plus the six requisites for successful menu planning arranged in the order C E A F B D, and the slogan 'Silbury's Soups are better because you taste each garden-fresh vegetable in every vitamin-rich spoonful' that had brought her on this Holiday of a Lifetime, Fifteen Days for Two on a Greek Island.

On the last posting date she had panicked and would have bought fifty-four more packets had it not been early closing day. Instead she sacrificed an unopened bottle of Mateus Rosé to Apollo by breaking it over the sundial, putting the splinters in the dustbin, and telling Mr Paton when he came back from the Rotary Club it had slipped out of her bad hand while she was dusting the cocktail cabinet.

At sunset, watching the sparrows swoop drunkenly over the lawn, she could have sworn she saw his dear golden face peeking at her out of a pink cloud.

Later when the letter came from Silbury's and Greece was in her grasp, Mr Paton had baulked. He brought out a brochure for the Golf Hotel, Nairn. He said he couldn't stand heat or history. The truth was, he was afraid. In a land where no one recognized his F.P. tie or understood his anecdotes he was as good as naked. She would have been sorry for him if she herself hadn't felt naked and foreign every day of her life.

She had come very near to leaving him over it. She had sat up all that night in her separate bed reading her paperback *Odyssey*, while he tossed and turned, complained about her bed lamp, tramped ostentatiously to the bathroom, rattled tumbler and sleeping tablets. By dawn she was ready to pack her case and go, well aware that the strength of her Hellenic passion compared with her lack of passion in other directions was as good as adulterous.

But over breakfast she found he had changed. Changed miraculously, while she herself was filled with quiet strength. He submitted to signing his passport application and the purchase of boxer shorts. They were here, together.

'And so they lived happily ever after,' declared Mrs Paton to the sky, and wondered at the cynicism in her voice.

The swimmy feeling that had driven her into the water had come back. She felt as light-headed as if she had drunk sherry before lunch. Light all over in fact. Her brain was acting quite irresponsibly, slipping away into an irritating state of euphoria instead of coming to grips with her condition. And when she tried to fight it, two syllables, repeated, pulsated somewhere just out of reach. She concentrated hard and caught an echo . . . RE-LAX, RE-LAX or was it LIE BACK, LIE BACK? The water lapping mesmerically in and around her ears whispered the offbeat. RE-re-LAX-lax LIE-lie-BACK-back.

'I *am* lying back,' she said. And so she was. Floating.

Flat on her back she marvelled at her expertise. But when she raised her head she rolled and toppled and broke the spell.

Relax, she told herself sternly, lie back. But it was difficult, heaving and gasping as her lungs fussily rejected the merest teaspoonful of sea water.

Steady and in command again, she took stock. Neither the hotel nor its brown rocks had been on her brief horizon.

She paddled cautiously through a forty-five degree turn, like one-sixteenth of a water lily that had Esther Williams as its pistil. The sun should be a guide but it seemed to be everywhere. She pictured herself a log, hoping that way to reduce sudden movement to a controlled roll. But when she raised her head this time her body separated into disorganized branches.

When she finished choking she had no sense of direction beyond up and down. Her panic was controlled by the need to stay steady, but she no longer flopped trustingly upon a polystyrene sea. The many drops of water temporarily united in supporting her spine were not to be relied on. Before plastic, before cellophane, before glass, density had gone hand in hand with opacity and transparent rightly meant fluid.

Something tickled her toes and brushed past her shoulder. She felt life and movement all about her and remembered the little fishes and the purple jellyfish.

She opened her eyes and saw again the seabird directly overhead, describing hypnotic figures, supporting itself easily on nothing. The thought steadied her.

She supposed the Greek Air Force ran an air-sea rescue service. The water was warm. At five Mr Paton would waken and look for her. But the fear stiffening under the bones of her swimsuit was not to be placated by clock-watching. From the rich store of her imagination she drew out an image and concentrated on it.

Alexander. This water had washed the keel of his ship. Maybe even now it was infinitesimally polluted with—er—pitch? Did they have pitch? Oil? Not mineral oil, of course, filthy stuff of dead seabirds and treble pink stamps. *Olive* oil. Pressed from the fruit and massaged into the hulls of beached ships by lovely laughing girls, the new wood glowing sherry and amber under the oil, the rich fruity smell of it, the silky swish of the girls' hands moving in rhythm over the curved hull . . .

Something familiar in the scene was distorting the picture. Ugh. Babies' bottoms and Olive Oil B.P. were getting in the way. She swallowed a crestful of wave, spluttered, and grappled with her vision control. Alexander. Concentrate on him.

Now Alexander stood alone on the deck of a wide ship, his back to the fiery wake and the setting sun. He yearned towards the East, and Mrs Paton yearned towards Alexander, when, all bright and burnished and beautiful, he turned to profile and urinated over the side. The water around her grew warm and pregnant with portent.

How *old* was water? Did it go off? It evaporated, of course, on the surface. Urine, being warm, should rise, but then, presumably being heavier than water, it would sink. But would it be heavier than *salt* water? Really there were times one wished one had paid attention in the Physics class. Even if it had evaporated, what went up must come down. But did it come down in the same place? It depended on the winds of course. Ye Gods . . . Alexander's urine could very well have rained on her garden in Portobello. Heavily diluted of course. Really, the thought was intolerable, the precious fluid disseminated amongst her neighbours' rhubarb. Altogether it was much more satisfactory to consider it preserved in the Aegean, and who was to prove otherwise? Let them try and she would confront them with the entire output of the classical heroes, Jason and Theseus and Achilles and Heracles, the sheer quantity of it defying evaporation and scepticism and marking this sea indelibly, for ever, buoyant and bubbling . . . so buoyant and bubbling . . . so wildly bubbling . . .

A slap, very twentieth century, as of wet plastic, caught her between the thighs. Revulsion blacked out her vision. She was struggling in a nightmare sea boiling with snorkels and flippers and shiny skin-diving suits and, between her legs, an inflated plastic duck, lifting her out of the water, her hands clutching, slipping, clasping about the neck of the creature, thick neck, heavy body, heavier than water, but floating. Not floating. Swimming. Muscles at work beneath the skin and blood coursing. Warm blood. Mammals. Suckle their young. Such as, for instance, the whale, the porpoise and the . . .

Mrs Paton drew herself upright and, assuming the pose of Artemis, head back, chest out, allowed the dolphin to carry her to the island.

He was waiting for her on the beach. She recognized him at once by his improbably erect beard and the thunderbolt on the table in front of him.

He rose to greet her, and she was fleetingly anxious, as if planted without notice in the Buckingham Palace line-up. How did one greet the King of the Gods?

He came closer and put his hands on her wet shoulders. She angled a cheek for a kiss—was it left or right first?—but he was no de Gaulle. He held her away and looked her slowly up and down, her varnished damaged toes, her pink satin one-piece, her shaven underarms, her wet yellow perm . . . could he find beauty in them, or dignity?

Mrs Paton inclined her head regally and was led to the table. She tugged modestly at her swimsuit and sat squelchily on the wooden chair which Zeus held for her. He sat opposite and still he did not speak.

The table was set with grapes and black olives, meat, and a terracotta pitcher of wine, and from this he filled a goblet for her and topped up his own. Hers, when she raised it, was decorated in the image of her host with a tallish lady. She looked at him over the rim.

'Cheers,' he said, and drank.

'Cheers,' she replied, badly shocked, and drank too, a second shock. The wine tasted like syrup of figs or British sherry. Could it be *nectar*? Cheers indeed.

The velvety accented voice spoke again.

'You flew by Olympic?'

'Yes.' Really. Next he'd be telling her he was a director.

'You will stay for two weeks—fifteen days—yes? That is usual.'

His 'yes?' had the startling ring of the Mediterranean tourist tout, a hawker of hire cars and straw hats and boat trips round the bay. She felt equal and opposite and took courage.

'Do you spend much time in the islands?'

'In summer, yes, though it gets harder to find an empty one. They come in their toy ships and swim around the shores with their rubber feet and their glass windows.

'Last week on the sacred island of Delos a girl from your land gave birth to a child. We felt the tremor on Olympus. Apollo visited the child with a disease and it died soon after. She had hair like a Maenad, the mother, and lived with others in a tent on the beach.'

'Hippies.'

'Please?'

'It's a general term for such people. They do no harm.'

Zeus snorted into his nectar and tore at some meat without offering her any. Mrs Paton took an olive in rebuke.

'Apollo is still alive then?'

'How could he be otherwise?'

She wanted to ask about Hera but it seemed indelicate. Zeus was wolfing the meat, chewing it with his mouth open, a habit she deplored. She must distract him before he took another mouthful. Politics, that was it. Greeks liked to talk politics.

'What do you think of the Revolutionary Government?'

'The Gods are above party politics.'

'But you must *think* about them?'

'Why? They never think of us. When our land was great it was not men who made it so. Not men unaided. They struggle now to find again the purpose of those days. They forget the purpose was never theirs.'

'Oh I do so agree,' said Mrs Paton. She had never voted, never expressed a political opinion in her life. She found it impossible to ally herself with the motives of her fellow men. People thought her stupid. But not Zeus. He listened most attentively as she outlined her philosophy, her conviction that society, not religion, was the opiate of the masses.

'People cling to each other because they are afraid to contemplate infinity,' she said. And he nodded and refilled her goblet.

She decided to tell him about the intolerable materialism of life in the twentieth century. Of the hideous seductions of the consumer world so that, however long you held out against them, in the end your horizons too became cluttered with dishwashers and you warmed your heart with central heating and double glazing because there was nothing else to hope for, nothing.

Zeus told her about Jason and the Golden Fleece and she listened politely. 'But the Fleece was only the Means,' she said. 'Double glazing is an End in itself.' And he had to agree.

She conjured for him the baying of the mob when you stepped outside it, the horror of bus parties where they made you sing, of staff dances and Woolworth's on Saturdays and Rothesay in July.

She described the country cottage she had found soon after her marriage, the thatch and the isolation and the long view over the moors, and the arbour where she planned to build a shrine to Apollo. He looked piqued.

Then she told him of the house they had bought instead, of how she had imagined they were building her tomb as she watched it grow, brick by ugly brick, till it looked like every other in the street.

'You won't need a tomb now,' said Zeus, filling her goblet again.

Tears dripped into the wine as she relived her honeymoon in Pitlochry, her futile pregnancy, her failure to make close friends or successful sponge cakes, her short romance with a poodle till she killed it with overfeeding.

'It is better so,' said Zeus. 'Your time must not be taken up with trivia.'

She talked and he listened till the sun was the flaky dull gold of an icon and the nectar a dying crescendo in her head.

She recalled her childhood. She had been an embarrassing child. They had had to carry her home from a matinee of *Snowhite* when she sobbed loudly at 'Some Day My Prince Will Come' and refused to be comforted by a choc ice. In her teens *The Flying Dutchman* had affected her the same way.

She had never fancied the local boys, nor indeed Mr Paton. She had held out stonily against the Dramatic Society and the church choir and the Townswomen's Guild.

'I always *knew* there was Something More,' she cried.

Zeus yawned, politely, behind his hand, and the gesture, so like Mr Paton's, plummeted her rudely back into the present.

'Oh dear,' she said, 'I have been going on. It must be the wine.' Indeed her face, when she touched it, was very hot, and her hair quite dishevelled and strawy.

'It *has* been nice meeting you,' she said, 'but I really must go.'

'No!' cried Zeus with an intensity that startled her. 'Not yet.' And a seabird, a grey seabird, swooped down on to a nearby rock and looked at them pointedly.

Zeus saw the bird too and his expression changed as he reached for something under the table. A parting gift? A statuette, maybe, or a nice vase?

It was a Japanese transistor set. How odd. He put it on the table between them and found some bouzouki music. Then he smiled at her. It was the first time he had smiled and it changed his face so dramatically it quite gave her the creeps.

'What is your name?'

'Phyllis.'

'Ph-y-ll-is.' The way he said it it might have been Desiree.

'I have waited for you a long time, Phyllis.'

'Really?'

'Poseidon combed the waves for you and Apollo swept the skies.'

'For me?'

'But it was foretold you would come along, stepping out of the waves on to the shore of this island we have kept for you.'

She looked about dazedly at the sand, the brown rocks, the small undistinguished hill that rose inland. Across the strait she could see another brown coastline with a white rectangle that must be the hotel.

'Why me?'

'Because you alone believe. On Olympus we felt your belief and grew strong because of it. Your sacrifices gave us the power to hope.'

She remembered the lamb cutlet, the handful of cornflakes tossed furtively into the Aga, the ear of barley picked in a field and laid out casually as for the birds.

'And now you are here as it was foretold. More beautiful by far than ever I had hoped, your hair as gold as never a mortal's that I saw before, your breasts two pink pillows, your . . .'

Inside, Mrs Paton began to freeze. Reflected in Zeus's eyes she saw a big pink middle-aged woman, gawky and diffident as a thirteen-year-old.

She tried to get up but her elbow collided with her goblet which emptied itself over the hand advancing towards her. Zeus licked it clean and began to fiddle with the transistor. Now Sinatra was competing with the bouzouki and some static, and his hands, both of them, were moving again across the table top. They were smooth, too smooth, and his breath smelt of garlic.

'Phyllis, lovely Phyllis, look at me.'

Mrs Paton blushed and fidgeted with the thunderbolt. It was small but heavy and her fingertips tingled when she touched it.

Zeus's hand, greasy with meat fat, came down purposefully on hers and she tingled all over.

'The time has come. All but two thousand years would pass, we knew, from the birth of him who turned man's minds from the Old Gods, till the coming of the New Mother . . .'

'*Mother?*'

Mrs Paton blushed right down under her swimsuit and tried to withdraw her hand. She failed. Her ears were ringing and softly through the din came the pulsating syllable . . . RE-LAX, RE-LAX, LIE BACK, LIE BACK . . . She shook her head to clear it. Zeus was still talking, holding her with his eye and his hand.

'Mother,' he was saying, 'mother of the first new God of the Second Coming, son of my Second Rule, seed of my loins, fruit of your womb . . .'

'*Stop it!*' screamed Mrs Paton and leaped to her feet, overturning the table. The thunderbolt slid on to the sand and the sky grew dark.

As the first crash shook the heavens the wine spilt itself sizzling upon the thunderbolt and the rain began. It tore at her uncovered flesh and she crossed her arms over her chest. The wind came and blew the shattered pitcher, the grapes, the olive stones, until the beach looked like a Sunday picnic spot under the primeval terror of the storm.

Whimpering, Mrs Paton stood first on one leg, then the other, tucking them up like a frantic flamingo to save them from the stinging sand. They were all the same, even Gods. There was no place for her in the world or in the universe. She was alone, hopeless, ugly, doomed, misjudged, violated. Apollo would never have treated her like this, nor Mr Paton.

'Greasy wop!' she screamed into the wind and abandoned herself to an ecstasy of self pity.

Zeus stood apart, powerless, his beard limp and dripping. Poseidon, helpless to intercede, raged around the world wrecking many ships. Hades beat his breast in fury and seismologists in many countries sent out warnings.

Only Sinatra remained unmoved, singing his little triumph from the wet sand, 'Love's been good to me.'

Zeus kicked the radio till he stopped.

'Cursed woman,' said Zeus to the seabird. 'I never had this trouble with the others.'

Athena shed her disguise and stood revealed in a white robe and gold sandals. Mrs Paton observed her secretly through her fingers as she snivelled and hiccuped.

'I can't think what went wrong,' Athena was saying. 'The wine, the music, the table for two, the good listening . . . That is the procedure. I have watched them. Perhaps you should have offered her presents? Money? Power?'

Zeus growled and the thunder echoed him. 'All-conquering Zeus does not bribe women. His favours are reward enough. And the prize of a place on Olympus.'

'What?' shouted Mrs Paton.

They turned to stare at her.

'Me? On Olympus?'

'Of course,' said Zeus. 'When I claim the child.'

Oh bliss. Oh joy. Oh vindication. Oh confusion to mortals. Home at last. Mrs Paton let out a sigh, a lifetime long.

Zeus raised his hand and the storm ceased.

And now Zeus and Mrs Paton stood alone on the beach.

'The child,' said Zeus, closing in, 'will go to Eton. I will claim him before the world on his eighteenth birthday.'

'And I will be truly immortal?'

'As I am,' said Zeus, yanking on her shoulder straps.

Mrs Paton fought him off. 'And I shall meet Apollo?'

'Yes yes,' said Zeus, discovering the miracle of the zip. But she had stopped fighting.

Afterwards, speeding back across the strait on the dolphin, Mrs Paton half expected to be chased by a gadfly. If she got through the next thirteen days it would be all right. Once back in Edinburgh Hera would find it hard to harry her. She must be on her guard against bolting horses and mad dogs. She doubted Hera would have the wit to adapt to speeding taxis, but if she did she had all the resources of the New World to pit against her.

Mr Paton was drinking ouzo on the terrace with Bill and Mavis, Lee and Sharon and the German couple, telling them about Edinburgh, the Athens of the North.

'Well well well,' he said, 'we were beginning to think you'd been struck by the lightning.'

'I was,' said Mrs Paton without blushing. ❦

George Mackay Brown

ANDRINA

Andrina comes to see me every afternoon in winter, just before it gets dark. She lights my lamp, sets the peat fire in a blaze, sees that there is enough water in my bucket that stands on the wall niche. If I have a cold (which isn't often, I'm a tough old seaman) she fusses a little, puts an extra peat or two on the fire, fills a stone hot-water bottle, puts an old thick jersey about my shoulders.

That good Andrina—as soon as she has gone, after her occasional ministrations to keep pleurisy or pneumonia away—I throw the jersey from my shoulders and mix myself a toddy, whisky and hot water and sugar. The hot-water bottle in the bed will be cold long before I climb into it, round about midnight: having read my few chapters of Conrad.

Towards the end of February last year I did get a very bad cold, the worst for years. I woke up, shuddering, one morning, and crawled between fire and cupboard, gasping like a fish out of water, to get a breakfast ready. (Not that I had an appetite.) There was a stone lodged somewhere in my right lung, that blocked my breath.

I forced down a few tasteless mouthfuls, and drank hot ugly tea. There was nothing to do after that but get back to bed with my book. Reading was no pleasure either—my head was a block of pulsing wood.

'Well,' I thought, 'Andrina'll be here in five or six hours' time. She won't be able to do much for me. This cold, or flu, or whatever it is, will run its course. Still, it'll cheer me to see the girl.'

Andrina did not come that afternoon. I expected her with the first cluster of shadows: the slow lift of the latch, the low greeting, the 'tut-tut' of sweet disapproval at some of the things she saw as soon as the lamp was burning. . . . I was, though, in that strange fatalistic mood that sometimes accompanies a fever, when a man doesn't really care what happens. If the house was to go on fire, he might think, 'What's this, flames?' and try to save himself: but it wouldn't horrify or thrill him.

I accepted that afternoon, when the window was blackness at last with a first salting of stars, that for some reason or another Andrina couldn't come. I fell asleep again.

I woke up. A gray light at the window. My throat was dry—there was a fire in my face—my head was more throbbingly wooden than ever. I got up, my feet flashing with cold pain on the stone floor, drank a cup of water, and climbed back into bed. My teeth actually clacked and chattered in my head for five minutes or more—a thing I had only read about before.

I slept again, and woke up just as the winter sun was making brief stained glass of sea and sky. It was, again, Andrina's time. Today there were things she could do for me: get aspirin from the shop, surround my grayness with three or four very hot bottles, mix the strongest toddy in the world. A few words from her would be like a bell-buoy to a sailor lost in a hopeless fog. She did not come.

She did not come again on the third afternoon.

I woke, tremblingly, like a ghost in a hollow stone. It was black night. Wind soughed in the chimney. There were, from time to time, spatters of rain against the window. It was the longest night of my life. I experienced, over again, some of the dull and sordid events of my life; one certain episode was repeated again and again like an ancient gramophone record being put on time after time, and a rusty needle scuttling over worn wax. The shameful images broke and melted at last into sleep. Love had been killed but many ghosts had been awakened.

When I woke up I heard, for the first time in four days, the sound of a voice. It was Stanley the postman speaking to the dog of Bighouse. 'There now, isn't that loud big words to say so early? It's just a letter for Minnie, a drapery catalogue. There's a good boy, go and tell Minnie I have a love letter for her. . . . Is that you, Minnie? I thought old Ben here was going to tear me in pieces then. Yes, Minnie, a fine morning, it is that. . . . '

I have never liked that postman—a servile lickspittle to anyone he thinks is of consequence in the island—but that morning he came past my window like a messenger of light. He opened the door without knocking (I am a person of small consequence). He said, 'Letter from a long distance, skipper.' He put the letter on the chair nearest the door. I was shaping my mouth to say, 'I'm not very well. I wonder. . . . ' If words did come out of my mouth, they must have been whispers, a ghost appeal. He looked at the dead fire and the closed window. He said, 'Phew! It's fuggy in here, skipper. You want to get some fresh air. . . . ' Then he went, closing the door behind him. (He would not, as I had briefly hoped, be taking word to Andrina, or the doctor down in the village.)

I imagined, until I drowsed again, Captain Scott writing his few last words in the Antarctic tent.

In a day or two, of course, I was as right as rain; a tough old salt like me isn't killed off that easily.

But there was a sense of desolation on me. It was as if I had been betrayed—deliberately kicked when I was down. I came almost to the verge of self-pity. Why had my friend left me in my bad time?

Then good sense asserted itself. 'Torvald, you old fraud,' I said to myself. 'What claim have you got, anyway, on a winsome twenty-year-old? None at all. Look at it this way, man—you've had a whole winter of her kindness and consideration. She brought a lamp into your dark time: ever since the Harvest Home when (like a fool) you had too much whisky and she supported you home and rolled you unconscious into bed. . . . Well, for some reason or another Andrina hasn't been able to come these last few days. I'll find out, today, the reason.'

It was high time for me to get to the village. There was not a crust or scraping of butter or jam in the cupboard. The shop was also the Post Office—I had to draw two weeks' pension. I promised myself a pint or two in the pub, to wash the last of that sickness out of me.

It struck me, as I trudged those two miles, that I knew nothing about Andrina at all. I had never asked, and she had said nothing. What was her father? Had she sisters and brothers? Even the district of the island where she lived had never cropped up in our talks. It was sufficient that she came every evening, soon after sunset, and performed her quiet ministrations, and lingered awhile; and left a peace behind—a sense that everything in the house was pure, as if it had stood with open doors and windows at the heart of a clean summer wind.

Yet the girl had never done, all last winter, asking me questions about myself—all the good and bad and exciting things that had happened to me. Of course I told her this and that. Old men love to make their past vivid and significant, to stand in relation to a few trivial events in as fair and bold a light as possible. To add spice to those bits of autobiography, I let on to have been a reckless wild daring lad—a known and somewhat feared figure in many a port from Hong Kong to Durban to San Francisco. I presented to her a character somewhere between Captain Cook and Captain Hook.

And the girl loved those pieces of mingled fiction and fact; turning the wick of my lamp down a little to make everything more mysterious, stirring the peats into new flowers of flame. . . .

One story I did not tell her completely. It is the episode in my life that hurts me whenever I think of it (which is rarely, for that time is locked up and the key dropped deep in the Atlantic: but it haunted me—as I hinted—during my recent illness).

On her last evening at my fireside I did, I know, let drop a hint or two to Andrina—a few half-ashamed half-boastful fragments. Suddenly, before I had finished—as if she could foresee and suffer the end—she had put a white look and a cold kiss on my cheek, and gone out at the door; as it turned out, for the last time.

Hurt or no, I will mention it here and now. You who look and listen are not Andrina—to you it will seem a tale of crude country manners: a mingling of innocence and heartlessness.

In the island, fifty years ago, a young man and a young woman came together. They had known each other all their lives up to then, of course—they had sat in the school room together—but on one particular day in early summer this boy from one croft and this girl from another distant croft looked at each other with new eyes.

After the midsummer dance in the barn of the big house, they walked together across the hill through the lingering enchantment of twilight—it is never dark then—and came to the rocks and the sand and sea just as the sun was rising. For an hour and more they lingered, tranced creatures indeed, beside those bright sighings and swirlings. Far in the north-east the springs of day were beginning to surge up.

It was a tale soaked in the light of a single brief summer. The boy and the girl lived, it seemed, on each other's heartbeats. Their parents' crofts were miles apart, but they contrived to meet, as if by accident, most days; at the crossroads, in the village shop, on the side of the hill. But really these places were too earthy and open— there were too many windows—their feet drew secretly night after night to the beach with its bird-cries, its cave, its changing waters. There no one disturbed their communings—the shy touches of hand and mouth—the words that were nonsense but that became in his mouth sometimes a sweet mysterious music—'Sigrid'.

The boy—his future, once this idyll of a summer was ended, was to go to the university in Aberdeen and there study to be a man of security and position and some leisure—an estate his crofting ancestors had never known.

No such door was to open for Sigrid—she was bound to the few family acres—the digging of peat—the making of butter and cheese. But for a short time only. Her place would be beside the young man with whom she shared her breath and heart-beats, once he had gained his teacher's certificate. They walked day after day beside shining beckoning waters.

But one evening, at the cave, towards the end of that summer, when the corn was taking a first burnish, she had something urgent to tell him—a tremulous perilous secret thing. And at once the summertime spell was broken. He shook his head. He looked away. He looked at her again as if she were some slut who had insulted him. She put out her hand to him, her mouth trembling. He thrust her away. He turned. He ran up the beach and along the sand-track to the road above; and the ripening fields gathered him soon and hid him from her.

And the girl was left alone at the mouth of the cave, with the burden of a greater more desolate mystery on her.

The young man did not go to any seat of higher learning. That same day he was at the emigration agents in Hamnavoe, asking for an urgent immediate passage to Canada or Australia or South Africa—anywhere.

Thereafter the tale became complicated and more cruel and pathetic still. The girl followed him as best she could to his transatlantic refuge a month or so later; only to discover that the bird had flown. He had signed on a ship bound for furthest ports, as an ordinary seaman: so she was told, and she was more utterly lost than ever.

That rootlessness, for the next half century, was to be his life: making salt circles about the globe, with no secure footage anywhere. To be sure, he studied his navigation manuals, he rose at last to be a ship's officer, and more. The barren years became a burden to him. There is a time, when white hairs come, to turn one's back on long and practised skills and arts, that have long since lost their savours. This the sailor did, and he set his course homeward to his island; hoping that fifty winters might have scabbed over an old wound.

And so it was, or seemed to be. A few remembered him vaguely. The name of a certain vanished woman—who must be elderly, like himself, now—he never mentioned, nor did he ever hear it uttered. Her parents' croft was a ruin, a ruckle of stones on the side of the hill. He climbed up to it one day and looked at it coldly. No sweet ghost lingered at the end of the house, waiting for a twilight summons—'Sigrid. . . .'

I got my pension cashed, and a basket full of provisions, in the village shop. Tina Stewart the postmistress knew everybody and everything; all the shifting subtle web of relationship in the island. I tried devious approaches with her. What was new or strange in the island? Had anyone been taken suddenly ill? Had anybody—a young woman, for example—had to leave the island suddenly, for whatever reason? The hawk eye of Miss Stewart regarded me long and hard. No, said she, she had never known the island quieter. Nobody had come or gone. 'Only yourself, Captain Torvald, has been bedridden, I hear. You better take good care of yourself, you all alone up there. There's still a grayness in your face. . . . ' I said I was sorry to take her time up. Somebody had mentioned a name—Andrina—to me, in a certain connection. It was a matter of no importance. Could Miss Stewart, however, tell me which farm or croft this Andrina came from?

Tina looked at me a long while, then shook her head. There was nobody of that name—woman or girl or child—in the island; and there never had been, to her certain knowledge.

I paid for my messages, with trembling fingers, and left.

I felt the need of a drink. At the bar counter stood Isaac Irving the landlord. Two fishermen stood at the far end, next the fire, drinking their pints and playing dominoes.

I said, after the third whisky, 'Look, Isaac, I suppose the whole island knows that Andrina—that girl—has been coming all winter up to my place, to do a bit of cleaning and washing and cooking for me. She hasn't been for a week now and more. Do you know if there's anything the matter with her?' (What I dreaded to hear was that Andrina had suddenly fallen in love; her little rockpools of charity and kindness drowned in that huge incoming flood; and had cloistered herself against the time of her wedding.)

Isaac looked at me as if I was out of my mind. 'A young woman,' said he. 'A young woman up at your house? A home help, is she? I didn't know you had a home help. How many whiskies did you have before you came here, skipper, eh?' And he winked at the two grinning fishermen over by the fire.

I drank down my fourth whisky and prepared to go.

'Sorry, skipper,' Isaac Irving called after me. 'I think you must have imagined that girl, whatever her name is, when the fever was on

27

you. Sometimes that happens. The only women I saw when I had the flu were hags and witches. You're lucky, skipper—a honey like Andrina!'

I was utterly bewildered. Isaac Irving knows the island and its people, if anything, even better than Tina Stewart. And he is a kindly man, not given to making fools of the lost and the delusion-ridden.

Going home, March airs were moving over the island. The sky, almost overnight, was taller and bluer. Daffodils trumpeted, silently, the entry of spring from ditches here and there. A young lamb danced, all four feet in the air at once.

I found, lying on the table, unopened, the letter that had been delivered three mornings ago. There was an Australian postmark. It had been posted in late October.

'I followed your young flight from Selskay half round the world, and at last stopped here in Tasmania, knowing that it was useless for me to go any farther. I have kept a silence too, because I had such regard for you that I did not want you to suffer as I had, in many ways, over the years. We are both old, maybe I am writing this in vain, for you might never have returned to Selskay; or you might be dust or salt. I think, if you are still alive and (it may be) lonely, that what I will write might gladden you, though the end of it is sadness, like so much of life. Of your child—our child—I do not say anything, because you did not wish to acknowledge her. But that child had, in her turn, a daughter, and I think I have seen such sweetness but rarely. I thank you that you, in a sense (though unwillingly), gave that light and goodness to my age. She would have been a lamp in your winter, too, for often I spoke to her about you and that long-gone summer we shared, which was, to me at least, such a wonder. I told her nothing of the end of that time, that you and some others thought to be shameful. I told her only things that came sweetly from my mouth. And she would say, often, 'I wish I knew that grandfather of mine. Gran, do you think he's lonely? I think he would be glad of somebody to make him a pot of tea and see to his fire. Some day I'm going to Scotland and I'm going to knock on his door, wherever he lives, and I'll do things for him. Did you love him very much, gran? He must be a good person, that old sailor, ever to have been loved by you. I *will* see him. I'll hear the old stories from his own mouth. Most of all, of course, the love story—for you, gran, tell me nothing about that. . . . ' I am writing this letter, Bill, to tell you that this can never now be. Our grand-daughter Andrina died last week, suddenly, in the first stirrings of spring. . . .'

Later, over the fire, I thought of the brightness and burgeoning and dew that visitant had brought across the threshold of my latest winter, night after night; and of how she had always come with the first shadows and the first star; but there, where she was dust, a new time was brightening earth and sea. ❧

A. L. Kennedy

TEA AND BISCUITS

I went to visit him, late because I had to drive slowly, but I ran all the stairs to make up. He opened the door and I'll tell you what we said.

'You smell the kettle boiling?'

'That's right.'

'Well, do come in.'

'Thank you. Thanks a lot.'

The flat was very like him; in his colours, with his books, his jacket on a chair in the living room. I recognised that. It was warm in there.

He must have been home for a while, sitting near the fire with the paper perhaps, and the sleeves of his shirt rolled up.

'Come and talk to me, then.'

'Hn?'

'I'll show my kitchen to you. Come on.'

I was wearing stockings. I like them, because they feel good, but I thought that he would like them, too. I didn't imagine he would see them, or that he would know I had them on, but I thought that he would like them if he did.

Nothing in his kitchen had names on, not even the coffee and tea. Some of it was in jars that you could see through, but for the rest, you would have to remember where everything was. There were ones that he always forgot: rice and porridge, oats and macaroni. I didn't know that then.

When Michael made us coffee he almost gave me sugar as if he expected I'd take it because he did. In the same way, later, I would see him pick up a book and feel it was strange when he didn't put glasses on.

I noticed, back in the living room, when he bent to turn down the fire, that the grey by his temples had faded to white. The cherry light from the gas shone round his head and the hairs that would be pale in daylight showed more red. He was no nearer balding than I remembered—hardly even thin—but his colours were changed, now. I saw that.

My grandfather was in hospital once, a long time ago. Very ill, and though nobody said so, I think he'd had a heart attack. I was taken to visit, just Gran and me, and I saw a stranger in his bed. He wore new, stripey cotton pyjamas. They were something from home and didn't suit the sheets. His head was low in the pillows and I could see his throat, soft and loose where he swallowed. Out of his shirt and pullover he wasn't like my grandfather at all. He was like anyone. Just a man lying down.

I kissed him goodbye and it felt like kissing a man. It felt funny, like when you think of Jesus or a minister being a man. It was like that. I felt guilty. I was seeing him in the way a stranger would. I was seeing his illness. I sat and looked at the bedspread and wasn't nice to him and left, knowing I'd let us both down.

I thought that in the morning our waking would be something like that. Between Michael and me. I thought that I would turn and look at him and see I had wasted it all, that an ageing man I'd once admired would be sleeping, maybe snoring at my side. He would smell of old sweat. I would see that the muscles in his arms were beginning to sink and be frightened by an old face, older in sleep. Slack.

I was wrong; selfish too. Probably selfish.

The warmth of his stomach was fitted against my back and his legs behind my legs were nice, just right. Perhaps his movement had disturbed me, I don't know, but however it happened, it was easy and that was me awake. I answered him with a voice I hadn't heard before, my thoughts running on and feeling new, and as I turned for his arm, I didn't doubt that I could look at him safely and find good. Something good would be there. I wanted him to see as much in me.

He kissed me, I think on the nose, and said 'Good morning.'

'Come here. I want to tell you. I love you.'

'That's nice.'

There are different and better ways to say it. Anything I've ever thought of has seemed to be second hand; something you might have stolen from Tammy Wynette. I should have said that when he ran, and he often did, he ran like nobody else and I loved him for that. He had a rhythm and blues kind of run. Pale socks. I should have said I loved him for every time, but most of all for my first, because he made it a gift and a thing to remember and he was sweet.

That morning was strange. We sat up in bed, recovering slowly, and looked at it and declared it all to be extremely odd. Herring gulls heading to sea again, flying soft and heavy up the street and a light behind the paper shop window, but no sound. The street lamps whispered out below us and the last of the night wore away while Michael brought me tea in bed as if I was somehow fragile after the night.

'How are you feeling?'

'Very nice.'

'You don't hurt?'

'No. I ache a bit.'

'Where?'

'You want me to show you?'

'I'm going to have trouble with you.'

I told him that I'd missed the Sixties, and I felt I had a lot to make up. All that permissiveness.

'You missed nothing. Move over, I'm getting cold.'

Perhaps what surprised us both was our luck. When I was still his student we could have tried it, had the affair, plenty of other people always did. There were even two or three times when it could have started, like when my father died and Michael was so nice. He told me that it wouldn't get better, but I could manage it a day at a time. He could have been more sympathetic and tried to get more in return. We could have let it happen then and lasted a couple of terms, maybe more. Meeting again, later, I could have been married, or he might not have been divorced, or something very small could have happened. The day we had coffee together one of us might have been nursing a cold, or been depressed and the chance would have gone. Instead we had been lucky.

All through the fogs and the drizzle, until the air became firmer and the marigolds abandoned at the close mouth were feathered every morning with white, all through it, we learned about us. I remembered how new Michael could be. I would catch him, some-times, smiling in a different light, or say goodbye to him and see him walk away and I would know there were things about him I hadn't begun to find out about yet. That pleased me.

Most of his past I knew, but I couldn't share. Some of the women I might have recognised in the street; certainly, if we'd had the chance to speak. I would have known the perfume, the way they liked to dress and, if they told me stories, I would have heard most of them before. There might be a new one, about this man with brown eyes and long hands who liked to keep chocolate in the fridge. At the end they would call him a bastard and look beyond my shoulder with a tired, short smile.

That was how I imagined it would be. I never had the chance to try. I never met his wife. His ex-wife. Although I wanted to. I wanted to see if she was like him in ways that I was; to see what they had left of each other, and perhaps what would happen to us. Just to set my mind at rest. I told him it might be alright. He said I was perverse, so there you go.

My past was easy. Very short. School: my school friends still in touch enough to have a drink at Christmas, or other times a coffee, if we met. Summer holidays and birthdays and fat-kneed boys in kilts at dances and, almost in spite of everything, no sex. Michael was surprised at that. Sometimes pleased and sometimes guilty, but always surprised at that. The university bit he knew, because he was there and because, like a few of the others, he took an interest in the people he taught. It hadn't been so long, he would tell us, since he was one of us. I had five years to fill him in on: unemployed, then selling insurance, melting down new candles for the MSC and then getting the job. It took me ten minutes to tell him. The picture of me as a baby on the lopsided rug, the yellow-haired, dead father and the mother, he knew all of that.

We announced ourselves to mother, later. Like this.

It happened in the daft days. The New Year was over and the holiday nearly done, a yellow oil of lamplight over the rainy streets. We should have arrived in the summer with light clothes and smiles. Instead our faces were numb and raw, our fingers blind with the cold. We needed to have her tea, to be comfortable by her fire, on the sofa and Father's chair. By the time we had our wits about us, Mother was ready.

'Go and fill the pot will you, darling?'

And away I went. I got back and she was interviewing Michael.

It wasn't that we hadn't expected it. It was a natural thing for her to do, but I wish that I could have said something when it happened. Something right. Instead I stood in the doorway, hardly listening, and thought of a book I'd found in Michael's flat. It was a hardback— Persian Art—I don't remember. And when I picked it out of the armchair to put it away I noticed a name and address and a date on the blank leaf at the front. It told me he had lived in a different city, in a house I didn't know and he had bought himself a book, priced in shillings when I was three years old. The nearest I can get to how I felt was how sad it was that he would die before me. How lonely I would be. I don't think, in her interview, mother ever mentioned that.

By the way, we hurt her. Not because of what we did, but because I hadn't told her. She hadn't known for all that time. I still saw her quite often with Michael and alone, but always she would speak to me as if I was a guest. She didn't trust herself to me; neither thought nor dream, and every time I saw her, she made me ashamed.

It was almost as if she had died and, perhaps because I had lost her or perhaps because of Mike, or both, I found that I wanted a child. I wanted to make it and have it, for it to be alive with the two of us.

My mother's pregnancy had ended very happily, laughing, in fact. Mother had been watching a new Woody Allen film, I suppose I could find out which one, and suddenly, in a silence, she laughed. She laughed and found she couldn't stop laughing. Her laughing made her laugh. The worry in the face of my father, the little crowd of usherettes, the rush of figures who took her from the back of the cinema to the ambulance; they all made her laugh.

She gave birth within the hour, one month early, still weeping and giggling, amazed, and thinking of that first, secret thing that started her laugh.

I was not born even smiling, only a little underweight.

I wanted a child. I wanted it born laughing, they wouldn't be allowed to make it cry. I would tell them and Mike would make sure. I would have asked him to. It would have been good.

Before the end, before I start on that, there are too many things that were good that I remember. Sitting here, the rungs of the bench are against my spine and a crowd of sparrows is rocking a holly tree, but, behind them, it is quiet. Very quiet. There is space.

I always seem to think of Michael in the kitchen. He is at his clearest then, perhaps because we were busy together there, visiting each other, interrupting, letting things boil. I can smell the wet earth from the potatoes, our red, clay soil. He takes oranges and orange scent from a brown paper bag.

'Fifty pence for five. That's not bad. They're big.'

'You're mean, you know that? I've noticed.'

'They're big oranges, look. I'm not mean.'

'You're stingy.'

'Nice, cheap oranges. I am not stingy.'

'You're a stingy, grouchy, old man.'

He was wearing the big coat, the blue one. It smelt of evening weather and the car. I slipped my arms inside it and around his waist. That was something I did a lot.

'You're just after my oranges.'

'That's right.'

Michael stood very still for a while. He said,

'You do make me happy sometimes. You don't know.'

The dinner was good, with oranges after.

If I'd come to the park last week the afternoon would have been longer, but evenings come in fast now. You can see the change from day to day. By the time I get home the lights will be in the windows and Michael will be back, the fires on. He doesn't like the house to be cold.

I will tell him then. I think I will tell him.

I went there because it's a public service. In the student days we came for the tea and biscuits, but it felt good afterwards, just the same. You knew you could have saved a life. You hadn't run into a burning building or pulled a child out of the sea, but part of you had been taken and it would help someone. I liked it when they laid you on your bed with so many other people, all on their beds, all together with something slightly nervous and peaceful in the air.

They would talk to you and find a vein, do it all so gently, and I would ask for the bag to hold as it filled. The nurse would rest it on my stomach and I would feel the weight in it growing and the strange warmth. It was a lovely colour, too. A rich, rich red. I told my mother about it and she laughed.

I gave them my blood a couple of times after that, then my periods made me anaemic and then I forgot. I don't know what made me go back to start again.

Nothing much had changed, only the form at the beginning which was different and longer and I lay on a bed in a bus near the shopping centre, not in a thin, wooden hall.

Afterwards they send you a certificate. It comes in the post and you get a little book to save them in, like co-op stamps. This time they sent me a letter instead. It was a kind, frightening letter which said I should come and see someone; there might be something wrong with my blood.

I am full of blood. My heart is there for moving blood. The pink under my fingernails is blood. I can't take it away.

And now I am not what I thought I was. I am waiting to happen. I have a clock now, they told me that. A drunk who no longer drinks is sober, but he has a clock because every new day might be the day that he slips. His past becomes his achievement, not his future. I have a clock like that. I look at my life backwards and all of it's winding down. I think that is how it will stay. I think that's it.

Should I say it to Michael like that? Should I tell him that thing I remember about the American tribe. Those Indians. They thought that we went through life on a river, all facing the stern of the boat and we only ever looked ahead in dreams. That's what I'll have to do now.

I think he told me about that. It sounds like him. It would give us some kind of start for the conversation. ❦

James Kelman

TEN GUITARS

They stopped outside the gates to the Nurses' Home. He could see the night-porter peering through the window trying to identify the girl. The rain pattered relentlessly but not too heavily, down on her umbrella. 'I better go in,' she said, with a half smile, staring in at the little porter's lodge.

'Thought you were allowed till twelve before the gates were shut?' he asked.

She shrugged without replying and, shuffling her feet, began humming a song to herself.

'Come on we'll walk up the road a bit where there are no spies.'

'Oh Danny doesn't bother.' She had stepped backwards into the shadows, expecting him to follow. The night-porter turned the page of a newspaper with his left hand; he held a tea cup against his cheek with the other. Perhaps she was right. He didn't appear the least bit interested.

'Fancy a coffee?'

'In your flat I suppose!' she smiled.

'Well it's only a room, but it's warm, and I've got a chair.'

'That's not what I mean.'

He turned his coat collar up before answering. 'Listen, if you know any cafes still open we'll go there.' He could not be bothered. What he did want to say was listen, why don't you go in or why don't you come out, I'm getting tired and really, what's the diff anyway? But she was always having to play little games all the time.

'I'm only kidding,' she said.

'Yeh,' he smiled. 'Sorry. Come on then, let's go and drink coffee, I'm too tired to rape you anyway.'

'Very funny!' she laughed briefly.

He had met her at the hospital dance four weeks ago and this was the sixth time they had been out together. Cinema twice. Pub thrice. This evening she hadn't finished until 8 o'clock so they had dined in an Indian restaurant, had a couple of drinks afterwards and strolled back in the rain. He didn't find her tremendously attractive but she seemed to quite like him. They had had no sex yet. At the beginning he had attempted to get it going but this was waning and now amounted to little more than jokes and funny remarks on the subject. She was half a head shorter than him, dressed quite well if six months behind in style, had short black hair and wore this brown corduroy coat he liked the first times but not so much now. She had a sharp wee upturned nose, was nineteen years old, kissed with sealed lips and came from Bristol.

'No females allowed in here you know!' he said, quietly turning the key in the lock of the outside door. 'Under any circumstances.'

She giggled, gazing up and down the street. 'I can only stay ten minutes,' she whispered, peering into the gloomy and musty smelling hallway.

Beckoning her to follow they crept upstairs without switching on any lights. This place was known as a respectable bachelors-only house. It was wholly maintained by an eighty-eight year old Italian lady who preferred older, retired if possible, gentlemen. She had only allowed him in through her husband whom he had met playing dominoes in the local pub. 'Steady boy,' he told his wife. But it was clean and quiet, and during the short while he had been staying he had only twice set eyes on another tenant. On another occasion, just after closing-time, somebody had bumped against his door and seemed to fall upstairs. When he investigated whoever it was had vanished. He had concluded that the person was living directly above but could not be sure. The rent was £3.50 a week for this medium sized room containing a mighty bed which resembled his idea of what an orthopaedic bed must look like. It was shaped like a small but steep hill; four feet high at the top and half that at the bottom. Occasionally he woke up with his feet sticking out over the end and his head about eighteen inches below the pillows. An unusual continental quilt covered it all. The interior of the mattress seemed to be stuffed with potato crisp packets and startling crinkling noises escaped whenever he turned onto his side. It was extremely comfortable! Although there was no running water, there was an old marble-topped table of some kind and an enormous jug and basin; underneath the table stood an enamel bucket, and all three vessels plus the battered electric kettle were filled daily with fresh water. There were no cooking facilities. Under no circumstances was cooking allowed in the house, even if he had gone out and bought his own cooker. The landlady was totally opposed to it. At first he would buy things like cheese and cold meat but recently he had discovered tinned frankfurters and boiled eggs. He emptied the frankfurters into the electric kettle and also one or two eggs. Once the water had boiled for three minutes the grub was ready for eating. The only snag was the actual kettle, which was a very old model. It had a tiny spout and a really wee opening on top, maybe less than three inches in diameter. This meant he had to spear the frankfurters out individually with a fork which required skill, frequently leaving bits of sausage floating about after; and often the eggs would crack when dropped down onto the kettle bottom which caused the water to become cobwebby from the escaping egg white. Fortunately the flavour of the coffee never seemed all that impaired. He was secretly proud of his ingenuity but was unable to display it to the girl having neither frankfurter nor egg. Still, she did seem pleased to get the chair and the coffee. He switched on the gas-fire.

'Very quiet,' she said presently.

'Haunted.'

She smiled her disbelief.

'You don't believe me? There's things go bump in the night here, I'm telling you.'

'I don't believe you.'

'Okay . . .' Sitting on the carpet he began twiddling the knobs on the transistor radio. 'What's Luxembourg again?'

'208 metres. If I believed everything you told me I'd go mad or something.'

'Doesn't bother me if you're too nervous to hear.' He switched off the radio and continued in a low growling kind of stage-voice. 'One dark winter's evening just after closing-time around the turn of the century, an aged retired navvy was returning home from the boozer . . .'

'Retired what?'

'Navvy. And he was still wearing his Wellingtons, returning from the boozer quietly singing this shanty to himself when he opened the front door and climbed the creaky stairs.' He paused and pointed at the door. 'Just as he passed that very door on his way up he stopped in terror. At the top he saw this death's head staring down at him. Well he staggered back letting out this blood curdling scream and went toppling down the stairs banging on that door as he went to his doom.'

'Did he?' she said politely.

'Yeh, really! They say to this day if you climb the stair occasionally just after closing-time you'll sometimes see a death's head wearing a pair of Wellington boots. I know it's hard to believe but there you are.'

She gazed above his head.

'Too much bloody interference at this time of night,' he muttered, back with the transistor radio. 'You want Radio 1?'

'There's nothing on after seven. I don't really mind.' She had begun humming this tune again to herself. Why the hell didn't she go! Sitting there like Raquel Welch. Anyway if she really did fancy him surely she'd want to kip up with him—at least for the night. Good Christ. And it was nearly 12 o'clock probably. Still, he didn't have to get up for work in the morning. But what would happen if they locked her out or something? Get chucked out the nurses' home? And he would get chucked out this place if Arrivederchi Roma found out.

'Want another coffee?'

'I don't mind.'

'Well yes or no?'

'If you're having one.'

'I'm not having one but if you want one just go ahead and say so.'

'I'm not fussy.'

Jesus why didn't she get up and go? 'Plenty of books there if you want a read . . . ' He gestured vaguely beneath the bed where a pile of paperbacks was lying.

'No thanks.'

He ripped a piece of newspaper and stuck it through the grill of the gas-fire to get a light for his cigarette, and said, 'Did you never smoke?'

'Yes, quite heavily, but I gave it up last Christmas.'

'Mmm, good for you. I sometimes . . . ' He lacked the energy to finish the sentence.

'There's jobs going in the hospital for storemen and porters,' she said.

'Is that right?'

'Yes, and they're earning good wages. The man you see is a Mister Harvey. They're desperate for staff.'

Perhaps she was only seeing him in an attempt to recruit him for the position of porter. She had begun humming that song again. He looked at her. 'What tune's that again?'

'*Ten Guitars*. I've always liked it. It was only a B side. My big sister had it.'

Wish to Christ she was here just now. 'No,' he said, 'I like the fast numbers myself.'

'You would,' she laughed. She actually laughed! What was this? A note of encouragement at long last. What was he supposed to do now? He had not that much desire to start playing around again, too bad on the nerves. Anyway, she didn't have the brains to drop hints. She didn't even have the brains to . . .

'What was that?' she cried.

'What?'

'That noise.' She stared at the door.

'Ssh. Might be that old one creeping about, checking up on everybody. If she finds you here I'm right in trouble.'

'Oh,' she replied, relieved.

'You didn't believe that death's head twaddle did you?'

'Of course not—I'm used to you by now.'

What did she mean by that? He stood to his feet and walked to the cupboard to get the alarm clock. He began to wind it up. After setting it down again he stared at the back of her shoulders as she stared at the gas-fire, humming that song to herself. He had to try once more. It was getting ridiculous. Stepping over to her chair he kissed the nape of her neck. She did not move. Her blouse fastened at the back and he unbuttoned the top buttons and fumbled at the hook on her bra.

'What d'you think you're playing at?' she asked.

'Nothing. I'm taking off your blouse, but I'm stuck.' Then he discovered the catch thing and added, 'No I'm not.' He continued on the blouse again and she allowed it to slide off her shoulders and then folded it up and placed it neatly on the carpet. Meanwhile he held both strap ends of the bra. But he had reached this point before in the alley behind the hospital, and on the very first night after the dance he had managed to get his fingertips beneath the rim of her pants. What had been going wrong since? He stepped round the chair to face her. He took both her hands and pulled her to her feet and kissed her. Still unsure but almost letting himself believe this could only be it. Then he paused. She unzipped her skirt at the side and walked out of it, and climbed onto the bed and under the quilt. She reached back and slung the bra over the back of the bed.

'Never seen one of these before,' she said, indicating the quilt and unaware of his incredulous stare.

'It's a continental quilt!' he answered at last. He was still dazed when he undressed, down to his socks and underpants. He went to switch off the light. She giggled.

'What's up?'

'You! in your socks and skinny legs.' She laughed again, a bit shrilly.

'Lucky it's not a pair of Wellingtons!' he grinned, nervously, and marched forward.

But he had forgotten to alter the usual going-off time on the alarm clock and it burst out at 10 a.m. as normal. Recognising the severity of the situation he jumped out of bed at once and dressed rapidly. The landlady rose at dawn and would have cleaned and exorcised the rest of the house by this time. Fortunately she wouldn't come into the room unless the door was open which he had to do first thing upon leaving every day. He told her to hurry up. What a confrontation if the old one burst through the door! 'Come on,' he whispered.

She found her pants among the fankle of sheets and quilt at the foot of the bed and quickly slipped them on. Attempting to pull up her tights she toppled onto the bed and giggled.

'Ssh for Christ sake—she's got ears like a fucking elephant.'

'No need to swear.'

'Sorry, but you better hurry.'

When finally she was ready he went out and then she did, and he closed the door gently. He looked upstairs and downstairs but no sign of the old one. Maybe out shopping or something! He was now standing on the first landing before the hallway. She came behind, clutching her coat and handbag. 'Got everything?' he asked.

She nodded, unable to speak.

He walked quickly and opened the outside door and peered up the street and down the street. No one! Grabbing her by the hand he tugged her down the seven steps to the pavement and they strode along the street in the direction opposite the one usually taken by the landlady.

Shortly after midday he returned. They had eaten breakfast then she had gone to get ready for duty, against his wishes. She always took her job very seriously. They had arranged to meet outside the hospital gates at eight that evening and he was really looking forward to it.

He walked upstairs and into his room and almost tripped over his suitcase which was parked right behind the door.

'Your goods all in there!' said the landlady, suddenly materialising in the doorway.

'What!'

'I'm not silly!' cried the old one. 'You had woman in my house last night. I pack in all your goods!'

'What? No, I didn't! A woman!'

'Come on, don't tell me. I know. I'm not silly!' She advanced towards him.

'Not me!' he protested, backing away.

'I tell Mister Pernacci no! I say no young man! But no! He say you are nice boy. Steady!' Her angular nose wrinkled in disgust. 'This the way you treat us eh?' She yelled.

He could only shrug. She was eighty-eight years of age at least.

'And Mister Clark say he hear noises other times. And I don't believe!'

'Ah he's a liar! Where does he live? Does he live up above?' He could not restrain a grin appearing on his face.

'Aah please please, do not be cheeky with me.'

'I'm not being cheeky. But it's not very nice throwing somebody out into the street like this is it?'

The landlady poked his back as she followed him downstairs. 'Don't talk,' she said, 'not very nice with woman in my house. Never before in many many years! Think of your mother! No, I think you never do that!'

'I'm a young man Missus Pernacci you must expect it.' He opened the door but paused. 'Surely you can at least think it over?'

'No. Come on. Out you go. Can't behave like this in people's houses!'

He shook his head.

'You must mend yourself,' she continued. 'Now please go. Mister Pernacci be very angry with you!'

'No he'll not!'

'Yes yes, he will.' Her old eyes widened at him. 'Now cheerio please.'

'Cheerio!' he called but the door slammed shut.

The rain was falling steadily when he came lugging the suitcase round the corner at 8 p.m. She was surprised to see it when she came out the gates. ❦

Susie Maguire

THE DAY I MET SEAN CONNERY

Nobody believes me. Nobody. They just give me the fish eye, and go 'oh yeah, right, Marina,' like I'm some wee kid that has to make up stories. Maybe they're just jealous, though. Maybe they'd never have had the nerve to actually do it? Like my friend Agnes, she goes mental if you mention Tom Cruise; or Veronica, she'd spend hours pulling her tights straight if there was a single chance in a million of getting close to Kevin Costner. Used to be it was Christian Slater, but Veronica's into older men now. The young ones are pathetic she says, and I've got to agree with her. Pathetic? They're hypothetical! Look at Tommy MacAuley, at her party, the way he stood in the hall smoking with all his stupid pals, and never once danced. See, older men have got past all that, and if you can put up with them being a bit bald or a bit fat, and having no clothes sense whatsoever, they're actually a lot more interesting, really.

Anyway, that's kinda how I feel about Sean. I've always thought he was brilliant, never mind that my mum used to drool over him in *Dr NO* and stuff, that never put me off. See, I think he's really got class—his wife being a painter, a bit of a John Bellany, kinda thing, all elongated and weird, and he seems to be wearing yellow v-necks in all her paintings, like he's just come off the golf course, and she's said 'freeze', or 'gelado' or whatever you say in Spanish. And that's another thing. Him speaking foreign languages. No way some young dipstick from Broxburn is going to take you to a restaurant and speak Spanish or Italian to the waiter. I dunno, just playing golf, and speaking Spanish, and having that deep voice and a great tan, and his really dry, very *very* dry humour, it all adds up, doesn't it? A perfect man.

Anyway, I was at the BBC in Glasgow, well, I went into the shop to get a Delia Smith book for my gran, and you had to go through reception, see? So I was just standing there, behind a couple of messenger guys with these huge Darth Vader helmets, who were flirting with the woman behind the desk—God, mutton dressed as lamb, all puffy sleeves and doo-dahs in her hair. So I sat down, right, they've got this TV, it's always turned to BBC, apparently, except at night, when the staff switch over to watch *Brookside*.

Anyway, it was on Ceefax, just going through these pages of news items, like about what a mess it was in England with all the floods, you know, and how fed up the insurance companies were about these sort of Acts of God, which serves them blooming right. They only really pay you any money when you die, and then what good does it do you?

Anyway, on the Ceefax it said blah blah blah Sean Connery, and I went OOOYAH, and read it quickly before the page changed. It was about him coming to Scotland to do a charity thing, a presentation, and it was going to be filmed by the BBC—today! And I looked around me, just casually, and nobody else had even noticed, they're all standing there in the exact same positions, looking bored, and Sean Connery is about to be in *the same building*! I couldn't believe it. And then I went—hang on, just hang on: what if I got to meet him? So I looked for a sign—you know, Ladies?—and decided I'd better go and look at myself in a mirror to see if the news had changed me, like my hair was standing on end, or my eyes had expanded or something.

Anyway, I went through these doors, and along a blue carpet in a blue corridor. People went by, but no one gave me looks, so I carried on, found the loo, went, and then put on a bit more make-up. I think eye-shadow makes me look like Jodie Foster in *Bugsy Malone*, but Veronica says it's sophisticated and mature, so I bunged on loads. Maybe they'd think I was Claire blooming Grogan, and give me a part in a play.

Anyway, I went back out, and wandered down a few more corridors, looking into offices as I passed—women typing, men talking on the phone. Typical. I found a lift, and went in and pushed a button, and got out one floor up. I turned left and found the cafeteria, which was quite empty, and I felt a bit nervous, but there was loads of really gorgeous looking food for about 5 p, so I had a vegetarian lasagne and salad and a coffee and a kit-kat, and found a newspaper, and sat and read and nibbled and sipped this dire coffee for about an hour. People kept going past with trays of this and that, amazing what people will eat, eh? Yoghurt and crisps? Is that a well-balanced meal? I bet these people get ulcers and die when they're forty-three, sitting in the dark all day in front of a VDU, eating crisps and yoghurt.

Anyway, four men came and sat down at a table nearby. All of them looked the same, they had big beards, greyish longish hair, denimey sort of shirts, like ZZ Top, but definitely not. They started talking about casting, and production costs, and stuff, so I suppose they must have been Producers or Directors or both. One of them would mention an actor, someone I'd heard of maybe, and the others would all go 'nah, too old, too fat, too young, too London, too Glasgow, his agent's a bitch. . . . ' They didn't agree about a single thing except that the coffee was weak, and that Scotland had no chance against Holland next Saturday. I was thinking about moving away when one of them said something about Sean. Then another one said, 'yeah, Craig's going to fetch him from the hotel about now, he'll be here for a 2 o'clock meeting', and the others all looked at their watches and sighed and moaned about work they had to catch up on, and they got up and started to leave. Blasé, or what? So I followed them, at least I followed the one who'd said all that about Craig. He trudged down dozens of stairs, and walked for miles and kept saying Hi to people. Eventually he went through this set of doors that said Studio Two, Silence, and all kinds of warnings about not going in if the light was red, but he had, so I followed. It was a huge, massive great place, with loads of people dragging lights around, and tiers of seating, and a big blonde woman wearing earmuff thingmies, standing on a stage area talking to herself—she kept saying, 'no, he's 6'2" and he's *not* wearing the rug' like it was a long-running argument with the Invisible Man.

Anyway, I took a notebook out of my bag, and stood in a dark corner, and tried to look official. The lights kept changing, and the monitors went on and off, and there were bits of old footage of Sean, looking absolutely divine, with this cool sharkskin suit on. And Sean's talking but I can't hear the words, though his voice is in my head going 'Up Perishcope, Up Perischcope', like in *Red October*. Oh God.

Anyway, just as I was looking at my watch and thinking '2.15 where is he', in he came—Sean. Mr Connery. He was dressed sort of casual but expensive, Pringle's best and a cap on his head. I suppose his head would be cold in Scotland, eh, after all the sun in

Marbella? There was a wee crowd round him, and I had this brilliant idea that if I just tagged along, maybe no one would notice. So that's exactly what I did. The minute they left the studio, I was on the trail, I'm telling you, it was V.I. blooming Warshawski—without the power dressing.

Anyway, all I could see of Sean was this cap, striding along out in front, with the grey-haired Producer guy I'd followed earlier nattering away at him about auto-cues and stuff. Sean's voice was a low rumble, monosyllabic, actually. He didn't sound very happy. We reached the lift, and Sean and the Producer slipped in, while the rest dithered, because it was obvious they couldn't all fit, but no one wanted to be the odd one out, so eventually the Producer said 'look, chaps and chapesses, meet us up in my office, okay?' and they all turned like sheep to go up the four flights of stairs. But I stuck my foot in the lift door, and smiled and said 'Going Up?'—honestly, I don't know where I got the nerve—and there I was, standing right next to Sean Connery. He was ginormous. I could have touched him, I could even have spent hours touching him, if the lift had got stuck, but it didn't. I just had a few minutes to gaze at the middle bits of him out of the corner of my eye, and take in the aftershave, and notice the freckles on the backs of his hands and then the lift stopped. I stood aside, and sort of waved my hand, meaning you go first, but he did that thing with his eyebrows that makes his nostrils flare, and said 'Ladiesh firsht' and I swear to God I nearly melted into a wee heap.

Anyway, I got my legs moving left right left right out of the lift, and then pretended to be really fascinated in this manky painting which had sort of twigs and stuff on it, not Joan Eardley, but some pathetic student rip-off merchant's idea of a winter landscape. I was keeping my ears open, as they went past me down another blue corridor and through a door at the bottom. All I heard was the words tea and make-up. I started to think, what am I doing here? What do I want? If I do get to talk to him, what am I going to say? and stuff like that. I didn't want to go in and ask for his autograph like some silly wee lassie, it had to be something else. Then I had a blinding revelation. Shortbread. He must really miss shortbread, in Marbella. I went pelting down the stairs to the first-floor canteen. I got a tray full of tea, coffee, real milk, sugar, and a huge plate of tartan-wrapped individual bits of shortbread. I carried it very very slowly to the lift, and went back up to the fourth floor, and down the corridor to Sean. I took a deep breath, and knocked on the door. He said 'Come in,' and I swear there was a wee lisp there, even on just those two words! So in I went, and he was sitting at a sort of Hollywood-style make-up table, with millions of light bulbs round it, in smart suit trousers and a white shirt, combing his moustache. Our eyes met through the mirror, and I nearly died. He said 'ah, tea'. 'Or coffee, if you'd rather,' I said. 'BBC coffee is always terrible,' he said, with this wee smile, and I nodded, like I knew what he meant, and I did. I poured him the tea, put the milk and sugar to hand, the teaspoon in the saucer, and pushed the plate of shortbread until it was practically under his chin. 'Bet you've not had this for a wee while,' I said. 'Go on, put some in your pocket for later, I always get peckish when I'm trying to go to sleep and have to sneak a biscuit.' I could hardly look at him, like I didn't want to actually see him, in case he disappeared. But he sort of laughed, and I did look, and he has these incredible eyes, dead crinkly, and deep, and it's like taking some powerful illegal substance or something, I just felt a big whoooosh—like: I Have Met Sean Connery and I Can Do Anything. Incredible. Magnetism. (I bet he could've made money as a hypnotist, if the film career hadn't panned out.)

Anyway. That was very nearly the last word I had with him, because right then the door opened and another tea-tray appeared. No shortbread. There was this big silence when the woman carrying it saw me, and then she just smiled and opened her mouth and shut it a few times, and finally inclined her head like she was conceding defeat, and backed out. My face must have told the story because Sean gave me a funny look. Then *he* poured *me* a cup of tea.

Anyway, I had to tell him, eventually. I just couldn't keep up the facade, you know. But he was very nice. He could've yelled, or phoned security or locked me in a cupboard, but he just looked at me, just—looked. And then he said 'why?' And I went 'why? Why, Sean? Don't you realise by now that there are millions of women who'll never meet anyone as good-looking as you, or as funny, that we're all going to have to settle for less? You're unique.' I probably went on a bit. I told him about myself, and my last boyfriend, and how we'd broken up, and how I didn't know if I should go to college. He raised the eyebrows and smiled like he was trying not to laugh. I didn't mind. It was great just having him there to talk to like a normal person. And he gave me lots of good advice, which I'm not going to pass on. He told me his golf handicap, and what he thought about Kevin Costner. I daren't tell Veronica. Finally, there was another knock on the door, and the grey-haired guy stuck his head through and went 'AAh AAh' and walked in sort of stiffly, rubbing his hands. And that's when I knew my time was up, so I stuck my hand out, and Sean stood up, and shook it, and said 'it was nice talking to you . . .' and I said 'Marina, Marina McLoughlin; very pleasant talking to you also, Sean.' Then he turned to the man, who had this sickly sort of grin on his puss and said 'Kenneth?' and I waved, and backed out of the door. And as soon as my legs un-wobbled, I made a run for it.

Anyway, that's the story about how I met Sean Connery. Veronica and Agnes aren't having it. I nearly phoned my ex-boyfriend, but you know, something stopped me, and I think it was the big whooosh I'd got off Sean. I thought no, I don't have to settle for less. Stuff Michael and his mountain bike and his bloody Gold Bier. I'm worth better. 🐛

Muriel Spark

A MEMBER OF THE FAMILY

'You must,' said Richard, suddenly, one day in November, 'come and meet my mother.'

Trudy, who had been waiting for a long time for this invitation, after all was amazed.

'I should like you,' said Richard, 'to meet my mother. She's looking forward to it.'

'Oh, does she know about me?'

'Rather,' Richard said.

'Oh!'

'No need to be nervous,' Richard said. 'She's awfully sweet.'

'Oh, I'm sure she is. Yes, of course, I'd love—'

'Come to tea on Sunday,' he said.

They had met the previous June in a lake town in Southern Austria. Trudy had gone with a young woman who had a bed-sitting-room in Kensington just below Trudy's room. This young woman could speak German, whereas Trudy couldn't.

Bleilach was one of the cheaper lake towns; in fact, cheaper was a way of putting it: it was cheap.

'Gwen, I didn't realize it ever rained here,' Trudy said on their third day. 'It's all rather like Wales,' she said, standing by the closed double windows of their room regarding the downpour and imagining the mountains which indeed were there, but invisible.

'You said that yesterday,' Gwen said, 'and it was quite fine yesterday. Yesterday you said it was like Wales.'

'Well, it rained a bit yesterday.'

'But the sun was shining when you said it was like Wales.'

'Well, so it is.'

'On a much larger scale, I should say,' Gwen said.

'I didn't realize it would be so wet.' Then Trudy could almost hear Gwen counting twenty.

'You have to take your chance,' Gwen said. 'This is an unfortunate summer.'

The pelting of the rain increased as if in confirmation.

Trudy thought, I'd better shut up. But suicidally: 'Wouldn't it be better if we moved to a slightly more expensive place?' she said.

'The rain falls on the expensive places too. It falls on the just and the unjust alike.'

Gwen was thirty-five, a schoolteacher. She wore her hair and her clothes and her bit of lipstick in such a way that, standing by the window looking out at the rain, it occurred to Trudy like a revelation that Gwen had given up all thoughts of marriage. 'On the just and the unjust alike,' said Gwen, turning her maddening imperturbable eyes upon Trudy, as if to say, you are the unjust and I'm the just.

Next day was fine. They swam in the lake. They sat drinking apple juice under the red-and-yellow awnings on the terrace of their guesthouse and gazed at the innocent smiling mountain. They paraded—Gwen in her navy blue shorts and Trudy in her puffy sunsuit—along the lake-side where marched also the lean brown camping youths from all over the globe, the fat print-frocked mothers and double-chinned fathers from Germany followed by their blonde sedate young, and the English women with their perms.

'There aren't any men about,' Trudy said.

'There are hundreds of men,' Gwen said, in a voice which meant, whatever do you mean?

'I really must try out my phrase-book,' Trudy said, for she had the feeling that if she were independent of Gwen as interpreter she might, as she expressed it to herself, have more of a chance.

'You might have more of a chance of meeting someone interesting that way,' Gwen said, for their close confinement by the rain had seemed to make her psychic, and she was continually putting Trudy's thoughts into words.

'Oh, I'm not here for that. I only wanted a rest, as I told you. I'm not—'

'Goodness, Richard!'

Gwen was actually speaking English to a man who was not apparently accompanied by a wife or aunt or sister.

He kissed Gwen on the cheek. She laughed and so did he. 'Well, well,' he said. He was not much taller than Gwen. He had dark crinkly hair and a small moustache of a light brown. He wore bathing trunks and his large chest was impressively bronze. 'What brings you here?' he said to Gwen, looking meanwhile at Trudy.

He was staying at an hotel on the other side of the lake. Each day for the rest of the fortnight he rowed over to meet them at ten in the morning, sometimes spending the whole day with them. Trudy was charmed, she could hardly believe in Gwen's friendly indifference to him, notwithstanding he was a teacher at the same grammar school as Gwen, who therefore saw him every day.

Every time he met them he kissed Gwen on the cheek.

'You seem to be on very good terms with him,' Trudy said.

'Oh. Richard's an old friend. I've known him for years.'

The second week, Gwen went off on various expeditions of her own and left them together.

'This is quite a connoisseur's place,' Richard informed Trudy, and he pointed out why, and in what choice way, it was so, and Trudy, charmed, saw in the peeling pastel stucco of the little town, the unnecessary floral balconies, the bulbous Slovene spires, something special after all. She felt she saw, through his eyes, a precious rightness in the women with their grey skirts and well-filled blouses who trod beside their husbands and their clean children.

'Are they all Austrians?' Trudy asked.

'No, some of them are German and French. But this place attracts the same type.'

Richard's eyes rested with appreciation on the young noisy campers whose tents were pitched in the lake-side field. The campers were long-limbed and animal, brightly and briefly dressed. They romped like galvanized goats, yet looked surprisingly virtuous.

'What are they saying to each other?' she inquired of Richard when a group of them passed by, shouting some words and laughing at each other through glistening red lips and very white teeth.

'They are talking about their fast M.G. racing cars.'

'Oh, have they got racing cars?'

'No, the racing cars they are talking about don't exist. Sometimes they talk about their film contracts which don't exist. That's why they laugh.'

'Not much of a sense of humour, have they?'

'They are of mixed nationalities, so they have to limit their humour to jokes which everyone can understand, and so they talk about racing cars which aren't there.'

Trudy giggled a little, to show willing. Richard told her he was thirty-five, which she thought feasible. She volunteered that she was not quite twenty-two. Whereupon Richard looked at her and looked away, and looked again and took her hand. For, as he told Gwen afterwards, this remarkable statement was almost an invitation to a love affair.

Their love affair began that afternoon, in a boat on the lake, when, barefoot, they had a game of placing sole to sole, heel to heel. Trudy squealed, and leaned back hard, pressing her feet against Richard's.

She squealed at Gwen when they met in their room later on. 'I'm having a heavenly time with Richard. I do so much like an older man.'

Gwen sat on her bed and gave Trudy a look of wonder. Then she said, 'He's not much older than you.'

'I've knocked a bit off my age,' Trudy said. 'Do you mind not letting on?'

'How much have you knocked off?'

'Seven years.'

'Very courageous,' Gwen said.

'What do you mean?'

'That you are brave.'

'Don't you think you're being a bit nasty?'

'No. It takes courage to start again and again. That's all I mean. Some women would find it boring.'

'Oh, I'm not an experienced girl at all,' Trudy said. 'Whatever made you think I was experienced?'

'It's true,' Gwen said, 'you show no signs of having profited by experience. Have you ever found it a successful tactic to remain twenty-two?'

'I believe you're jealous,' Trudy said. 'One expects this sort of thing from most older women, but somehow I didn't expect it from you.'

'One is always learning,' Gwen said.

Trudy fingered her curls. 'Yes, I have got a lot to learn from life,' she said, looking out of the window.

'God,' said Gwen, 'you haven't begun to believe that you're still twenty-two, have you?'

'Not quite twenty-two is how I put it to Richard,' Trudy said, 'and yes, I do feel it. That's my point. I don't feel a day older.'

The last day of their holidays Richard took Trudy rowing on the lake, which reflected a grey low sky.

'It looks like Windermere today, doesn't it?' he said.

Trudy had not seen Windermere, but she said, yes it did, and gazed at him with shining twenty-two-year-old eyes.

'Sometimes this place,' he said, 'is very like Yorkshire, but only when the weather's bad. Or, over on the mountain side, Wales.'

'Exactly what I told Gwen,' Trudy said. 'I said Wales, I said, it's like Wales.'

'Well, of course, there's quite a difference, really. It—'

'But Gwen simply squashed the idea. You see, she's an older woman, and being a schoolmistress—it's so much different when a man's a teacher—being a woman teacher, she feels she can treat me like a kid. I suppose I must expect it.'

'Oh well—'

'How long have you known Gwen?'

'Several years,' he said. 'Gwen's all right, darling. A great friend of my mother, is Gwen. Quite a member of the family.'

Trudy wanted to move her lodgings in London but she was prevented from doing so by a desire to be near Gwen, who saw Richard daily at school, and who knew his mother so well. And therefore Gwen's experience of Richard filled in the gaps in his life which were unknown to Trudy and which intrigued her.

She would fling herself into Gwen's room. 'Gwen, what d'you

think? There he was waiting outside the office and he drove me home, and he's calling for me at seven, and next week-end . . .'

Gwen frequently replied, 'You are out of breath. Have you got heart trouble?'—for Gwen's room was only on the first floor. And Trudy was furious with Gwen on these occasions for seeming not to understand that the breathlessness was all part of her only being twenty-two, and excited by the boy-friend.

'I think Richard's so exciting,' Trudy said. 'It's difficult to believe I've only known him a month.'

'Has he invited you home to meet his mother?' Gwen inquired.

'No—not yet. Oh, do you think he will?'

'Yes, I think so. One day I'm sure he will.'

'Oh, do you mean it?' Trudy flung her arms girlishly round Gwen's impassive neck.

'When is your father coming up?' Gwen said.

'Not for ages, if at all. He can't leave Leicester just now, and he hates London.'

'You must get him to come and ask Richard what his intentions are. A young girl like you needs protection.'

'Gwen, don't be silly.'

Often Trudy would question Gwen about Richard and his mother.

'Are they well off? Is she a well-bred woman? What's the house like? How long have you known Richard? Why hasn't he married before? The mother, is she—'

'Lucy is a marvel in her way,' Gwen said.

'Oh, do you call her Lucy? You must know her awfully well.'

'I'm quite,' said Gwen, 'a member of the family in my way.'

'Richard has often told me that. Do you go there *every* Sunday?'

'Most Sundays,' Gwen said. 'It is often very amusing, and one sometimes sees a fresh face.'

'Why,' Trudy said, as the summer passed and she had already been away for several week-ends with Richard, 'doesn't he ask me to meet his mother? If my mother were alive and living in London I know I would have asked him home to meet her.'

Trudy threw out hints to Richard. 'How I wish you could meet my father. You simply must come up to Leicester in the Christmas holidays and stay with him. He's rather tied up in Leicester and never leaves it. He's an insurance manager. The successful kind.'

'I can't very well leave Mother at Christmas,' Richard said, 'but I'd love to meet your father some other time.' His tan had worn off, and Trudy thought him more distinguished and at the same time more unattainable than ever.

'I think it only right,' Trudy said in her young way, 'that one should introduce the man one loves to one's parents'—for it was agreed between them that they were in love.

But still, by the end of October, Richard had not asked her to meet his mother.

'Does it matter all that much?' Gwen said.

'Well, it would be a definite step forward,' Trudy said. 'We can't go on being just friends like this. I'd like to know where I stand with him. After all, we're in love and we're both free. Do you know, I'm beginning to think he hasn't any serious intentions after all. But if he asked me to meet his mother it would be a sort of sign, wouldn't it?'

'It certainly would,' Gwen said.

'I don't even feel I can ring him up at home until I've met his mother. I'd feel shy of talking to her on the phone. I must meet her. It's becoming a sort of obsession.'

'It certainly is,' Gwen said. 'Why don't you just say to him, "I'd like to meet your mother"?'

'Well, Gwen, there are some things a girl can't say.'

'No, but a woman can.'

'Are you going on about my age again? I tell you, Gwen, I feel twenty-two. I think twenty-two. I am twenty-two so far as Richard's concerned. I don't think really you can help me much. After all, you haven't been successful with men yourself, have you?'

'No,' Gwen said, 'I haven't. I've always been on the old side.'

'That's just my point. It doesn't get you anywhere to feel old and think old. If you want to be successful with men you have to hang on to your youth.'

'It wouldn't be worth it at the price,' Gwen said, 'to judge by the state you're in.'

Trudy started to cry and ran to her room, presently returning to ask Gwen questions about Richard's mother. She could rarely keep away from Gwen when she was not out with Richard.

'What's his mother really like? Do you think I'd get on with her?'

'If you wish I'll take you to see his mother one Sunday.'

'No, no,' Trudy said. 'It's got to come from him if it has any meaning. The invitation must come from Richard.'

Trudy had almost lost her confidence, and in fact had come to wonder if Richard was getting tired of her, since he had less and less time to spare for her, when unexpectedly and yet so inevitably, in November, he said, 'You must come and meet my mother.'

'Oh!' Trudy said.

'I should like you to meet my mother. She's looking forward to it.'

'Oh, does she know about me?'

'Rather.'

'Oh!'

'It's happened. Everything's all right,' Trudy said breathlessly.

'He has asked you home to meet his mother,' Gwen said without looking up from the exercise book she was correcting.

'It's important to me, Gwen.'

'Yes, yes,' Gwen said.

'I'm going on Sunday afternoon,' Trudy said. 'Will you be there?'

'Not till supper time,' Gwen said. 'Don't worry.'

'He said, "I want you to meet Mother. I've told her all about you."'

'All about you?'

'That's what he said, and it means so much to me, Gwen. So much.'

Gwen said, 'It's a beginning.'

'Oh, it's the beginning of everything. I'm sure of that.'

Richard picked her up in his Singer at four on Sunday. He seemed preoccupied. He did not, as usual, open the car door for her, but slid into the driver's seat and waited for her to get in beside him. She fancied he was perhaps nervous about her meeting his mother for the first time.

The house on Campion Hill was delightful. They must be very *comfortable*, Trudy thought. Mrs Seeton was a tall, stooping woman, well dressed and preserved, with thick steel-grey hair and large light eyes. 'I hope you'll call me Lucy,' she said. 'Do you smoke?'

'I don't,' said Trudy.

'Helps the nerves,' said Mrs Seeton, 'when one is getting on in life. You don't need to smoke yet awhile.'

'No,' Trudy said. 'What a lovely room, Mrs Seeton.'

'*Lucy*,' said Mrs Seeton.

'Lucy,' Trudy said, very shyly, and looked at Richard for support. But he was drinking the last of his tea and looking out of the window as if to see whether the sky had cleared.

'Richard has to go out for supper,' Mrs Seeton said, waving her cigarette holder very prettily. 'Don't forget to watch the time, Richard. But Trudy will stay to supper with me, I *hope*. Trudy and I have a lot to talk about, I'm sure.' She looked at Trudy and very faintly, with no more than a butterfly-flick, winked.

Trudy accepted the invitation with a conspiratorial nod and a slight squirm in her chair. She looked at Richard to see if he would say where he was going for supper, but he was gazing up at the top pane of the window, his fingers tapping on the arm of the shining Old Windsor chair on which he sat.

Richard left at half-past six, very much more cheerful in his going than he had been in his coming.

'Richard gets restless on a Sunday,' said his mother.

'Yes, so I've noticed,' Trudy said, so that there should be no mistake about who had been occupying his recent Sundays.

'I dare say now you want to hear all about Richard,' said his mother in a secretive whisper, although no one was in earshot. Mrs Seeton giggled through her nose and raised her shoulders all the way up her long neck till they almost touched her earrings.

Trudy vaguely copied her gesture. 'Oh, yes,' she said, 'Mrs Seeton.'

'Lucy. You must call me Lucy, now, you know. I want you and me to be friends. I want you to feel like a member of the family. Would you like to see the house?'

She led the way upstairs and displayed her affluent bedroom, one wall of which was entirely covered by mirror, so that, for every photograph on her dressing-table of Richard and Richard's late father, there were virtually two photographs in the room.

'This is Richard on his pony, Lob. He adored Lob. We all adored Lob. Of course, we were in the country then. This is Richard with Nana. And this is Richard's father at the outbreak of war. What did you do in the war, dear?'

'I was at school,' Trudy said, quite truthfully.

'Oh, then you're a teacher, too?'

'No, I'm a secretary. I didn't leave school till after the war.'

Mrs Seeton said, looking at Trudy from two angles, 'Good gracious me, how deceiving. I thought you were about Richard's age, like Gwen. Gwen is such a dear. This is Richard as a graduate. Why he went into schoolmastering I don't know. Still, he's a very good master. Gwen always says so, quite definitely. Don't you adore Gwen?'

'Gwen is a good bit older than me,' Trudy said, being still upset on the subject of age.

'She ought to be here any moment. She usually comes for supper. Now I'll show you the other rooms and Richard's room.'

When they came to Richard's room his mother stood on the threshold and, with her finger to her lips for no apparent reason, swung the door open. Compared with the rest of the house this was a bleak, untidy, almost schoolboy's room. Richard's green pyjama trousers lay on the floor where he had stepped out of them. This was a sight familiar to Trudy from her several week-end excursions with Richard, of late months, to hotels up the Thames valley.

'So untidy,' said Richard's mother, shaking her head woefully. 'So untidy. One day, Trudy, dear, we must have a real chat.'

Gwen arrived presently, and made herself plainly at home by going straight into the kitchen to prepare a salad. Mrs Seeton carved slices of cold meat while Trudy stood and watched them both, listening to a conversation between them which indicated a long intimacy. Richard's mother seemed anxious to please Gwen.

'Expecting Grace tonight?' Gwen said.

'No, darling, I thought perhaps *not tonight*. Was I right?'

'Oh, of course, yes. Expecting Joanna?'

'Well, as it's Trudy's *first* visit, I thought perhaps not—'

'Would you,' Gwen said to Trudy, 'lay the table, my dear? Here are the knives and forks.'

Trudy bore these knives and forks into the dining-room with a sense of having been got rid of with a view to being talked about.

At supper, Mrs Seeton said, 'It seems a bit odd, there only being the three of us. We usually have such jolly Sunday suppers. Next week, Trudy, you must come and meet the whole crowd—mustn't she, Gwen?'

'Oh yes,' Gwen said, 'Trudy must do that.'

Towards half-past ten Richard's mother said, 'I doubt if Richard will be back in time to run you home. Naughty boy, I daren't think what he gets up to.'

On the way to the bus stop Gwen said, 'Are you happy now that you've met Lucy?'

'Yes, I think so. But I think Richard might have stayed. It would have been nice. I dare say he wanted me to get to know his mother by myself. But in fact I felt the need of his support.'

'Didn't you have a talk with Lucy?'

'Well yes, but not much really. Richard probably didn't realize you were coming to supper. Richard probably thought his mother and I could have a heart-to-heart—'

'I usually go to Lucy's on Sunday,' Gwen said.

'Why?'

'Well, she's a friend of mine. I know her ways. She amuses me.'

During the week Trudy saw Richard only once, for a quick drink.

'Exams,' he said. 'I'm rather busy, darling.'

'Exams in November? I thought they started in December.'

'Preparation for exams,' he said. 'Preliminaries. Lots of work.' He took her home, kissed her on the cheek and drove off.

She looked after the car, and for a moment hated his moustache. But she pulled herself together and, recalling her youthfulness, decided she was too young really to judge the fine shades and moods of a man like Richard.

He picked her up at four o'clock on Sunday.

'Mother's looking forward to seeing you,' he said. 'She hopes you will stay for supper.'

'You won't have to go out, will you, Richard?'

'Not tonight, no.'

But he did have to go out to keep an appointment of which his mother reminded him immediately after tea. He had smiled at his mother and said, 'Thanks.'

Trudy saw the photograph album, then she heard how Mrs Seeton had met Richard's father in Switzerland, and what Mrs Seeton had been wearing at the time.

At half-past six the supper party arrived. These were three women, including Gwen. The one called Grace was quite pretty, with a bewildered air. The one called Iris was well over forty and rather loud in her manner.

'Where's Richard tonight, the old cad?' said Iris.

'How do I know?' said his mother. 'Who am I to ask?'

'Well, at least he's a hard worker during the week. A brilliant teacher,' said doe-eyed Grace.

'Middling as a schoolmaster,' Gwen said.

'Oh, Gwen! Look how long he's held down the job,' his mother said.

'I should think,' Grace said, 'he's wonderful with the boys.'

'Those Shakespearian productions at the end of the summer term are really magnificent,' Iris bawled. 'I'll hand him that, the old devil.'

'Magnificent,' said his mother. 'You must admit, Gwen—'

'Very middling performances,' Gwen said.

'I suppose you are right, but, after all, they are only schoolboys. You can't do much with untrained actors, Gwen,' said Mrs Seeton very sadly.

'I adore Richard,' Iris said, 'when he's in his busy, occupied mood. He's so—'

'Oh yes,' Grace said, 'Richard is wonderful when he's got a lot on his mind.'

'I know,' said his mother. 'There was one time when Richard had just started teaching—I must tell you this story—he . . . '

Before they left Mrs Seeton said to Trudy, 'You will come with Gwen next week, won't you? I want you to regard yourself as one of us. There are two other friends of Richard's I do want you to meet. Old friends.'

On the way to the bus Trudy said to Gwen, 'Don't you find it dull going to Mrs Seeton's every Sunday?'

'Well, yes, my dear young thing, and no. From time to time one sees a fresh face, and then it's quite amusing.'

'Doesn't Richard ever stay at home on a Sunday evening?'

'No, I can't say he does. In fact, he's very often away for the whole week-end. As you know.'

'Who are these women?' Trudy said, stopping in the street.

'Oh, just old friends of Richard's.'

'Do they see him often?'

'Not now. They've become members of the family.' 🌢

Eric Linklater

SEALSKIN TROUSERS

I am not mad. It is necessary to realize that, to accept it as a fact about which there can be no dispute. I have been seriously ill for some weeks, but that was the result of shock. A double or conjoint shock: for as well as the obvious concussion of a brutal event, there was the more dreadful necessity of recognizing the material evidence of a happening so monstrously implausible that even my friends here, who in general are quite extraordinarily kind and understanding, will not believe in the occurrence, though they cannot deny it or otherwise explain—I mean explain away—the clear and simple testimony of what was left.

I, of course, realized very quickly what had happened, and since then I have more than once remembered that poor Coleridge teased his unquiet mind, quite unnecessarily in his case, with just such a possibility; or impossibility, as the world would call it. 'If a man could pass through Paradise in a dream,' he wrote, 'and have a flower presented to him as a pledge that his soul had really been there, and if he found that flower in his hand when he awoke—Ay, and what then?'

But what if he had dreamt of Hell and wakened with his hand burnt by the fire? Or of Chaos, and seen another face stare at him from the looking-glass? Coleridge does not push the question far. He was too timid. But I accepted the evidence, and while I was ill I thought seriously about the whole proceeding, in detail and in sequence of detail. I thought, indeed, about little else. To begin with, I admit, I was badly shaken, but gradually my mind cleared and my vision improved, and because I was patient and persevering—that needed discipline—I can now say that I know what happened. I have indeed, by a conscious intellectual effort, *seen and heard* what happened. This is how it began . . .

How very unpleasant! she thought.

She had come down the great natural steps on the seacliff to the ledge that narrowly gave access, round the angle of it, to the western face which today was sheltered from the breeze and warmed by the afternoon sun. At the beginning of the week she and her fiancé, Charles Sellin, had found their way to an almost hidden shelf, a deep veranda sixty feet above the white-veined water. It was rather bigger than a billiard-table and nearly as private as an abandoned light-house. Twice they had spent some blissful hours there. She had a good head for heights, and Sellin was indifferent to scenery. There had been nothing vulgar, no physical contact, in their bliss together on this oceanic gazebo, for on each occasion she had been reading Héaloin's *Studies in Biology* and he Lenin's *What is to be Done?*

Their relations were already marital, not because their mutual passion could brook no pause, but rather out of fear lest their friends might despise them for chastity and so conjecture some oddity or impotence in their nature. Their behaviour, however, was very decently circumspect, and they already conducted themselves, in public and out of doors, as if they had been married for several years. They did not regard the seclusion of the cliffs as an opportunity for secret embracing, but were content that the sun should warm and colour their skin; and let their anxious minds be soothed by the surge and cavernous colloquies of the sea. Now, while Charles was writing letters in the little fishing-hotel a mile away, she had come back to their sandstone ledge, and Charles would join her in an hour or two. She was still reading *Studies in Biology*.

But their gazebo, she perceived, was already occupied, and occupied by a person of the most embarrassing appearance. He was quite unlike Charles. He was not only naked, but obviously robust, brown-hued, and extremely hairy. He sat on the very edge of the rock, dangling his legs over the sea, and down his spine ran a ridge of hair like the dark stripe on a donkey's back, and on his shoulder-blades grew patches of hair like the wings of a bird. Unable in her disappointment to be sensible and leave at once, she lingered for a moment and saw to her relief that he was not quite naked. He wore trousers of a dark brown colour, very low at the waist, but sufficient to cover his haunches. Even so, even with that protection for her modesty, she could not stay and read biology in his company.

To show her annoyance, and let him become aware of it, she made a little impatient sound; and turning to go, looked back to see if he had heard.

He swung himself round and glared at her, more angry on the instant than she had been. He had thick eyebrows, large dark eyes, a broad snub nose, a big mouth. 'You're Roger Fairfield!' she exclaimed in surprise.

He stood up and looked at her intently. 'How do you know?' he asked.

'Because I remember you,' she answered, but then felt a little confused, for what she principally remembered was the brief notoriety he had acquired, in his final year at Edinburgh University, by swimming on a rough autumn day from North Berwick to the Bass Rock to win a bet of five pounds.

The story had gone briskly round the town for a week, and everybody knew that he and some friends had been lunching, too well for caution, before the bet was made. His friends, however, grew quickly sober when he took to the water, and in a great fright informed the police, who called out the lifeboat. But they searched in vain, for the sea was running high, until in calm water under the shelter of the Bass they saw his head, dark on the water, and pulled him aboard. He seemed none the worse for his adventure, but the police charged him with disorderly behaviour and he was fined two pounds for swimming without a regulation costume.

'We met twice,' she said, 'once at a dance and once in Mackie's when we had coffee together. About a year ago. There were several of us there, and we knew the man you came in with. I remember you perfectly.'

He stared the harder, his eyes narrowing, a vertical wrinkle dividing his forehead. 'I'm a little short-sighted too,' she said with a nervous laugh.

'My sight's very good,' he answered, 'but I find it difficult to recognize people. Human beings are so much alike.'

'That's one of the rudest remarks I've ever heard!'

'Surely not?'

'Well, one does like to be remembered. It isn't pleasant to be told that one's a nonentity.'

He made an impatient gesture. 'That isn't what I meant, and I do recognize you now. I remember your voice. You have a distinctive voice and a pleasant one. F sharp in the octave below middle C is your note.'

'Is that the only way in which you can distinguish people?'

'It's as good as any other.'

'But you don't remember my name?'

'No,' he said.

'I'm Elizabeth Barford.'

He bowed and said, 'Well, it was a dull party, wasn't it? The occasion, I mean, when we drank coffee together.'

'I don't agree with you. I thought it was very amusing, and we all enjoyed ourselves. Do you remember Charles Sellin?'

'No.'

'Oh, you're hopeless,' she exclaimed. 'What is the good of meeting people if you're going to forget all about them?'

'I don't know,' he said. 'Let us sit down, and you can tell me.'

He sat again on the edge of the rock, his legs dangling, and looking over his shoulder at her, said, 'Tell me: what is the good of meeting people?'

She hesitated, and answered, 'I like to make friends. That's quite natural, isn't it?—But I came here to read.'

'Do you read standing?'

'Of course not,' she said, and smoothing her skirt tidily over her knees, sat down beside him. 'What a wonderful place this is for a holiday. Have you been here before?'

'Yes, I know it well.'

'Charles and I came a week ago. Charles Sellin, I mean, whom you don't remember. We're going to be married, you know. In about a year, we hope.'

'Why did you come here?'

'We wanted to be quiet, and in these islands one is fairly secure against interruption. We're both working quite hard.'

'Working!' he mocked. 'Don't waste time, waste your life instead.'

'Most of us have to work, whether we like it or not.'

He took the book from her lap, and opening it read idly a few lines, turned a dozen pages and read with a yawn another paragraph.

'Your friends in Edinburgh,' she said, 'were better-off than ours.

Charles and I, and all the people we know, have got to make our living.'

'Why?' he asked.

'Because if we don't we shall starve,' she snapped.

'And if you avoid starvation—what then?'

'It's possible to hope,' she said stiffly, 'that we shall be of some use in the world.'

'Do you agree with this?' he asked, smothering a second yawn, and read from the book:

> The physical factor in a germ-cell is beyond our analysis, or assessment, but can we deny subjectivity to the primordial initiatives? It is easier, perhaps, to assume that mind comes late in development, but the assumption must not be established on the grounds that we can certainly deny self-expression to the cell. It is common knowledge that the mind may influence the body both greatly and in little unseen ways; but how it is done, we do not know. Psychobiology is still in its infancy.

'It's fascinating, isn't it?' she said.

'How do you propose,' he asked, 'to be of use to the world?'

'Well, the world needs people who have been educated— educated to think—and one does hope to have a little influence in some way.'

'Is a little influence going to make any difference? Don't you think that what the world needs is to develop a new sort of mind? It needs a new primordial directive, or quite a lot of them, perhaps. But psychobiology is still in its infancy, and you don't know how such changes come about, do you? And you can't foresee when you *will* know, can you?'

'No, of course not. But science is advancing so quickly—'

'In fifty thousand years?' he interrupted. 'Do you think you will know by then?'

'It's difficult to say,' she answered seriously, and was gathering her thoughts for a careful reply when again he interrupted, rudely, she thought, and quite irrelevantly. His attention had strayed from her and her book to the sea beneath, and he was looking down as though searching for something. 'Do you swim?' he asked.

'Rather well,' she said.

'I went in just before high water, when the weed down there was all brushed in the opposite direction. You never get bored by the sea, do you?'

'I've never seen enough of it,' she said. 'I want to live on an island, a little island, and hear it all round me.'

'That's very sensible of you,' he answered with more warmth in his voice. 'That's uncommonly sensible for a girl like you.'

'What sort of a girl do you think I am?' she demanded, vexation in her accent, but he ignored her and pointed his brown arm to the horizon: 'The colour has thickened within the last few minutes. The sea was quite pale on the skyline, and now it's a belt of indigo. And the writing has changed. The lines of foam on the water, I mean. Look at that! There's a submerged rock out there, and always, about half an hour after the ebb has started to run, but more clearly when there's an off-shore wind, you can see those two little whirlpools and the circle of white round them. You see the figure they make? It's like this, isn't it?'

With a splinter of stone he drew a diagram on the rock.

'Do you know what it is?' he asked. 'It's the figure the Chinese call the T'ai Chi. They say it represents the origin of all created things. And it's the sign manual of the sea.'

'But those lines of foam must run into every conceivable shape,' she protested.

'Oh, they do. They do indeed. But it isn't often you can read them.

There he is!' he exclaimed, leaning forward and staring into the water sixty feet below. 'That's him, the old villain!'

From his sitting position, pressing hard down with his hands and thrusting against the face of the rock with his heels, he hurled himself into space, and straightening in mid-air broke the smooth green surface of the water with no more splash than a harpoon would have made. A solitary razorbill, sunning himself on a shelf below, fled hurriedly out to sea, and half a dozen white birds, startled by the sudden movement, rose in the air crying 'Kittiwake! Kittiwake!'

Elizabeth screamed loudly, scrambled to her feet with clumsy speed, then knelt again on the edge of the rock and peered down. In the slowly heaving clear water she could see a pale shape moving, now striped by the dark weed that grew in tangles under the flat foot of the rock, now lost in the shadowy deepness where the tangles were rooted. In a minute or two his head rose from the sea, he shook bright drops from his hair, and looked up at her, laughing. Firmly grasped in his right hand, while he trod water, he held up an enormous blue-black lobster for her admiration. Then he threw it on to the flat rock beside him, and swiftly climbing out of the seat, caught it again and held it, cautious of its bite, till he found a piece of string in his trouser-pocket. He shouted to her, 'I'll tie its claws, and you can take it home for your supper!'

She had not thought it possible to climb the sheer face of the cliff, but from its forefoot he mounted by steps and handholds invisible from above, and pitching the tied lobster on to the floor of the gazebo, came nimbly over the edge.

'That's a bigger one than you've ever seen in your life before,' he boasted. 'He weighs fourteen pounds, I'm certain of it. Fourteen pounds at least. Look at the size of his right claw! He could crack a coconut with that. He tried to crack my ankle when I was swimming an hour ago, and got into his hole before I could catch him. But I've caught him now, the brute. He's had more than twenty years of crime, that black boy. He's twenty-four or twenty-five by the look of him. He's older than you, do you realize that? Unless you're a lot older than you look. How old are you?'

But Elizabeth took no interest in the lobster. She had retreated until she stood with her back to the rock, pressed hard against it, the palms of her hands fumbling on the stone as if feeling for a secret lock or bolt that might give her entrance into it. Her face was white, her lips pale and tremulous.

He looked round at her, when she made no answer, and asked what the matter was.

Her voice was faint and frightened. 'Who are you?' she whispered, and the whisper broke into a stammer. 'What are you?'

His expression changed and his face, with the waterdrops on it, grew hard as a rock shining undersea. 'It's only a few minutes,' he said, 'since you appeared to know me quite well. You addressed me as Roger Fairfield, didn't you?'

'But a name's not everything. It doesn't tell you enough.'

'What more do you want to know?'

Her voice was so strained and thin that her words were like the shadow of words, or words shivering in the cold: 'To jump like that, into the sea—it wasn't human!'

The coldness of his face wrinkled to a frown. 'That's a curious remark to make.'

'You would have killed yourself if—if—'

He took a seaward step again, looked down at the calm green depths below, and said, 'You're exaggerating, aren't you? It's not much more than fifty feet, sixty perhaps, and the water's deep.— Here, come back! Why are you running away?'

'Let me go!' she cried. 'I don't want to stay here. I—I'm frightened.'

'That's unfortunate. I hadn't expected this to happen.'

'Please let me go!'

'I don't think I shall. Not until you've told me what you're frightened of.'

'Why,' she stammered, 'why do you wear fur trousers?'

He laughed, and still laughing caught her round the waist and pulled her towards the edge of the rock. 'Don't be alarmed,' he said. 'I'm not going to throw you over. But if you insist on a conversation about trousers, I think we should sit down again. Look at the smoothness of the water, and its colour, and the light in the depths of it: have you ever seen anything lovelier? Look at the sky: that's calm enough, isn't it? Look at that fulmar sailing past: he's not worrying, so why should you?'

She leaned away from him, all her weight against the hand that held her waist, but his arm was strong and he seemed unaware of any strain on it. Nor did he pay attention to the distress she was in—she was sobbing dryly, like a child who has cried too long—but continued talking in a light and pleasant conversational tone until the muscles of her body tired and relaxed, and she sat within his enclosing arm, making no more effort to escape, but timorously conscious of his hand upon her side so close beneath her breast.

'I needn't tell you,' he said, 'the conventional reasons for wearing trousers. There are people, I know, who sneer at all conventions, and some conventions deserve their sneering. But not the trouser-convention. No, indeed! So we can admit the necessity of the garment, and pass to consideration of the material. Well, I like sitting on rocks, for one thing, and for such a hobby this is the best stuff in the world. It's very durable, yet soft and comfortable. I can slip into the sea for half an hour without doing it any harm, and when I come out to sun myself on the rock again, it doesn't feel cold and clammy. Nor does it fade in the sun or shrink with the wet. Oh, there are plenty of reasons for having one's trousers made of stuff like this.'

'And there's a reason,' she said, 'that you haven't told me.'

'Are you quite sure of that?'

She was calmer now, and her breathing was controlled. But her face was still white, and her lips were softly nervous when she asked him, 'Are you going to kill me?'

'Kill you? Good heavens, no! Why should I do that?'

'For fear of my telling other people.'

'And what precisely would you tell them?'

'You know.'

'You jump to conclusions far too quickly: that's your trouble. Well, it's a pity for your sake, and a nuisance for me. I don't think I can let you take that lobster home for your supper after all. I don't, in fact, think you will go home for your supper.'

Her eyes grew dark again with fear, her mouth opened, but before she could speak he pulled her to him and closed it, not asking leave, with a roughly occludent kiss.

'That was to prevent you from screaming. I hate to hear people scream,' he told her, smiling as he spoke. 'But this'—he kissed her again, now gently and in a more protracted embrace—'that was because I wanted to.'

'You mustn't!' she cried.

'But I have,' he said.

'I don't understand myself! I can't understand what has happened—'

'Very little yet,' he murmured.

'Something terrible has happened!'

'A kiss? Am I so repulsive?'

'I don't mean that. I mean something inside me. I'm not—at least I think I'm not—I'm not frightened now!'

'You have no reason to be.'

'I have every reason in the world. But I'm not! I'm not frightened—but I want to cry.'

'Then cry,' he said soothingly, and made her pillow her cheek against his breast. 'But you can't cry comfortably with that ridiculous contraption on your nose.'

He took from her the horn-rimmed spectacles she wore, and threw them into the sea.

'Oh!' she exclaimed. 'My glasses!—Oh, why did you do that? Now I can't see. I can't see at all without my glasses!'

'It's all right,' he assured her. 'You really won't need them. The refraction,' he added vaguely, 'will be quite different.'

As if this small but unexpected act of violence had brought to the boiling-point her desire for tears, they bubbled over, and because she threw her arms about him in a sort of fond despair, and snuggled close, sobbing vigorously still, he felt the warm drops trickle down his skin, and from his skin she drew into her eyes the saltness of the sea, which made her weep the more. He stroked her hair with a strong but soothing hand, and when she grew calm and lay still in his arms, her emotion spent, he sang quietly to a little enchanting tune a song that began:

> 'I am a Man upon the land,
>   I am a Selkie in the sea,
> And when I'm far from every strand
>   My home it is on Sule Skerry.'

After the first verse or two she freed herself from his embrace, and sitting up listened gravely to the song. Then she asked him, 'Shall I ever understand?'

'It's not a unique occurrence,' he told her. 'It has happened quite often before, as I suppose you know. In Cornwall and Brittany and among the Western Isles of Scotland; that's where people have always been interested in seals, and understood them a little, and where seals from time to time have taken human shape. The one thing that's unique in our case, in my metamorphosis, is that I am the only seal-man who has ever become a Master of Arts of Edinburgh University. Or, I believe, of any university. I am the unique and solitary example of a sophisticated seal-man.'

'I must look a perfect fright,' she said. 'It was silly of me to cry. Are my eyes very red?'

'The lids are a little pink—not unattractively so—but your eyes are as dark and lovely as a mountain pool in October, on a sunny day in October. They're much improved since I threw your spectacles away.'

'I needed them, you know. I feel quite stupid without them. But tell me why you came to the University—and how? How could you do it?'

'My dear girl—what is your name, by the way? I've quite forgotten.'

'Elizabeth!' she said angrily.

'I'm so glad, it's my favourite human name. But you don't really want to listen to a lecture on psychobiology?'

'I want to know *how*. You must tell me!'

'Well, you remember, don't you, what your book says about the primordial initiatives. But it needs a footnote there to explain that they're not exhausted till quite late in life. The germ-cells, as you know, are always renewing themselves, and they keep their initiatives though they nearly always follow the chosen pattern except in the case of certain illnesses, or under special direction. The direction of the mind, that is. And the glands have got a lot to do in a full metamorphosis, the renal first and then the pituitary, as you would expect. It isn't approved of—making the change, I mean— but every now and then one of us does it, just for a frolic in the general way, but in my case there was a special reason.'

'Tell me,' she said again.

'It's too long a story.'

'I want to know.'

'There's been a good deal of unrest, you see, among my people in the last few years: doubt, and dissatisfaction with our leaders, and scepticism about traditional beliefs—all that sort of thing. We've had a lot of discussion under the surface of the sea about the nature of man, for instance. We had always been taught to believe certain things about him, and recent events didn't seem to bear out what our teachers told us. Some of our younger people got dissatisfied, so I volunteered to go ashore and investigate. I'm still considering the report I shall have to make, and that's why I'm living, at present, a double life. I come ashore to think, and go back to the sea to rest.'

'And what do you think of us?' she asked.

'You're interesting. Very interesting indeed. There are going to be some curious mutations among you before long. Within three or four thousand years, perhaps.'

He stooped and rubbed a little smear of blood from his shin. 'I scratched it on a limpet,' he said. 'The limpets, you know, are the same today as they were four hundred thousand years ago. But human beings aren't nearly so stable.'

'Is that your main impression, that humanity's unstable?'

'That's part of it. But from our point of view there's something much more upsetting. Our people, you see, are quite simple creatures, and because we have relatively few beliefs, we're very much attached to them. Our life is a life of sensation—not entirely, but largely—and we ought to be extremely happy. We were, so long as we were satisfied with sensation and a short undisputed creed. We have some advantages over human beings, you know. Human beings have to carry their own weight about, and they don't know how blissful it is to be unconscious of weight: to be wave-borne, to float on the idle sea, to leap without effort in a curving wave, and look up at the dazzle of the sky through a smother of white water, or dive so easily to the calmness far below and take a haddock from the weed-beds in a sudden rush of appetite. Talking of haddocks,' he said, 'it's getting late. It's nearly time for fish. And I must give you some instruction before we go. The preliminary phase takes a little while, about five minutes for you, I should think, and then you'll be another creature.'

She gasped, as though already she felt the water's chill, and whispered, 'Not yet! Not yet, please.'

He took her in his arms, and expertly, with a strong caressing hand, stroked her hair, stroked the roundness of her head and the back of her neck and her shoulders, feeling her muscles moving to his touch, and down the hollow of her back to her waist and hips. The head again, neck, shoulders, and spine. Again and again. Strongly and firmly his hand gave her calmness, and presently she whispered, 'You're sending me to sleep.'

'My God!' he exclaimed, 'you mustn't do that! Stand up, stand up, Elizabeth!'

'Yes,' she said, obeying him. 'Yes, Roger. Why did you call yourself Roger? Roger Fairfield?'

'I found the name in a drowned sailor's pay-book. What does that matter now? Look at me, Elizabeth!'

She looked at him, and smiled.

His voice changed, and he said happily, 'You'll be the prettiest seal between Shetland and the Scillies. Now listen. Listen carefully.'

He held her lightly and whispered in her ear. Then kissed her on the lips and cheek, and bending her head back, on the throat. He looked, and saw the colour come deeply into her face.

'Good,' he said. 'That's the first stage. The adrenalin's flowing nicely now. You know about the pituitary, don't you? That makes it easy then. There are two parts in the pituitary gland, the anterior and posterior lobes, and both must act together. It's not difficult, and I'll tell you how.'

Then he whispered again, most urgently, and watched her closely. In a little while he said, 'And now you can take it easy. Let's sit down and wait till you're ready. The actual change won't come till we go down.'

'But it's working,' she said, quietly and happily. 'I can feel it working.'

'Of course it is.'

She laughed triumphantly, and took his hand.

'We've got nearly five minutes to wait,' he said.

'What will it be like? What shall I feel, Roger?'

'The water moving against your side, the sea caressing you and holding you.'

'Shall I be sorry for what I've left behind?'

'No, I don't think so.'

'You didn't like us, then? Tell me what you discovered in the world.'

'Quite simply,' he said, 'that we had been deceived.'

'But I don't know what your belief had been.'

'Haven't I told you?—Well, we in our innocence respected you because you could work, and were willing to work. That seemed to us truly heroic. We don't work at all, you see, and you'll be much happier when you come to us. We who live in the sea don't struggle to keep our heads above water.'

'All my friends worked hard,' she said. 'I never knew anyone who was idle. We had to work, and most of us worked for a good purpose; or so we thought. But you didn't think so?'

'Our teachers had told us,' he said, 'that men endured the burden of human toil to create a surplus of wealth that would give them leisure from the daily task of breadwinning. And in their hard-won leisure, our teachers said, men cultivated wisdom and charity and the fine arts; and became aware of God.—But that's not a true description of the world, is it?'

'No,' she said, 'that's not the truth.'

'No,' he repeated, 'our teachers were wrong, and we've been deceived.'

'Men are always being deceived, but they get accustomed to learning the facts too late. They grow accustomed to deceit itself.'

'You are braver than we, perhaps. My people will not like to be told the truth.'

'I shall be with you,' she said, and took his hand. But still he stared gloomily at the moving sea.

The minutes passed, and presently she stood up and with quick fingers put off her clothes. 'It's time,' she said.

He looked at her, and his gloom vanished like the shadow of a cloud that the wind has hurried on, and exultation followed like sunlight spilling from the burning edge of a cloud. 'I wanted to punish them,' he cried, 'for robbing me of my faith, and now, by God, I'm punishing them hard. I'm robbing their treasury now, the inner vault of all their treasury!—I hadn't guessed you were so beautiful! The waves when you swim will catch a burnish from you, the sand will shine like silver when you lie down to sleep, and if you can teach the red sea-ware to blush so well, I shan't miss the roses of your world.'

'Hurry,' she said.

He, laughing softly, loosened the leather thong that tied his trousers, stepped out of them, and lifted her in his arms. 'Are you ready?' he asked.

She put her arms round his neck and softly kissed his cheek. Then with a great shout he leapt from the rock, from the little veranda, into the green silk calm of the water far below . . .

I heard the splash of their descent—I am quite sure I heard the splash—as I came round the corner of the cliff, by the ledge that leads to the little rock veranda, our gazebo, as we called it, but the first thing I noticed, that really attracted my attention, was an enormous blue-black lobster, its huge claws tied with string, that was moving in a rather ludicrous fashion towards the edge. I think it fell over just before I left, but I wouldn't swear to that. Then I saw her book, the *Studies in Biology*, and her clothes.

Her white linen frock with the brown collar and the brown belt, some other garments, and her shoes were all there. And beside them, lying across her shoes, was a pair of sealskin trousers.

I realized immediately, or almost immediately, what had happened. Or so it seems to me now. And if, as I firmly believe, my apprehension was instantaneous, the faculty of intuition is clearly more important than I had previously supposed. I have, of course, as I said before, given the matter a great deal of thought during my recent illness, but the impression remains that I understood what had happened in a flash, to use a common but illuminating phrase. And no one, need I say? has been able to refute my intuition. No one, that is, has found an alternative explanation for the presence, beside Elizabeth's linen frock, of a pair of sealskin trousers.

I remember also my physical distress at the discovery. My breath, for several minutes I think, came into and went out of my lungs like the hot wind of a dust-storm in the desert. It parched my mouth and grated in my throat. It was, I recall, quite a torment to breathe. But I had to, of course.

Nor did I lose control of myself in spite of the agony, both mental and physical, that I was suffering. I didn't lose control till they began to mock me. Yes, they did, I assure you of that. I heard his voice quite clearly, and honesty compels me to admit that it was singularly sweet and the tune was the most haunting I have ever heard. They were about forty yards away, two seals swimming together, and the evening light was so clear and taut that his voice might have been the vibration of an invisible bow across its coloured bands. He was singing the song that Elizabeth and I had discovered in an album of Scottish music in the little fishing-hotel where we had been living:

'I am a Man upon the land,
I am a Selkie in the sea,
And when I'm far from any strand
I am at home on Sule Skerry!'

But his purpose, you see, was mockery. They were happy, together in the vast simplicity of the ocean, and I, abandoned to the terror of life alone, life among human beings, was lost and full of panic. It was then I began to scream. I could hear myself screaming, it was quite horrible. But I couldn't stop. I had to go on screaming . . . 🖤

Janice Galloway

WHERE YOU FIND IT

Nobody kisses like Derek.

First sight you think he's got no mouth, just a dry slit in that sheet face, lips that don't look like they'd sustain much at all, like worm husks, little worms rolled flat with no juice left in but you'd be wrong. When Derek kisses he opens up so wide you think he's choking on something, like he's trying to swallow an apple or maybe there's one stuck in his neck someplace and you open up too. He opens up like he's in the dentist's chair and you *know* you're being kissed. What he wants is to work his tongue in, he likes it deep and moving around in there, filling up all the room in your face. You can feel the tight little cord that keeps his tongue on stretching, pulling up from the soft palate like it might uproot. That soft little sliver is in there all the time, folded up like a fin or stray slice of tissue left on a butcher's tray, like something loveless left over from ritual surgery and on most people that's how it stays. You'd never suspect. When Derek kisses, though, you get a share of everything, you get it all. Sometimes it's scary like he's sucking me in, drawing me in deep so I can hardly breathe but I manage ok. I never push him away and I never, ever gag. That reflex thing where you think you're going to throw up? Even if he touches the back of my throat, the bit that's sheer like a toad's belly, I just don't do it because it's not that kind of thing, not like a punter sticking his dick there the way some of them do, some of them not even careful, not even bothered if it hurts or anything, not bothered about your vocal cords or anything, it's not like that. It's wonderful, the way he wants you to feel all of him in there, the root of this other tongue with taste buds reading like braille saying I AM KISSING YOU NOW. I love my own tongue having to make room for itself, pressing against his teeth, finding out the peach fur in the distant corners of his molars, the places no-one sees. I know all his secrets, even those bits of him, even bits he doesn't see. I like having no option about that, no choice. He just lifts those big square hands out of the blue, tangles the fingers up in my hair and tugs so my neck tilts for him without my sayso and injects himself. Without warning. And it's that, the fact he'll do it anywhere, that makes me weak. Even in the street he'll squeeze me open and take what he needs, like he just can't wait for me at all. There's no woman wouldn't love that, being wanted in a way that doesn't hide itself, a way that can't be shy. He doesn't want to fuck me. He doesn't even want to touch me anywhere else. Kisses are what I'm for he says. They're our thing, how he keeps me in line and I wouldn't let any other bastard do it, not even if they ask, not even if they're good looking and offer extra, I don't care. I'm all his. Derek's. Good kissers don't grow on trees. It's worth bearing in mind. You don't get everything in this life, girl, count your blessings. Remember the things he can do with his mouth. ❦

Bernard MacLaverty

A PORNOGRAPHER WOOS

I am sitting on the warm sand with my back to a rock watching you, my love. You have just come from a swim and the water is still in beads all over you, immiscible with the suntan oil. There are specks of sand on the thickening folds of your waist. The fine hairs on your legs below the knee are black and slicked all the one way with the sea. Now your body is open to the sun, willing itself to a deeper brown. You tan well by the sea. Your head is turned away from the sun into the shade of your shoulder and occasionally you open one eye to check on the children. You are wearing a black bikini. Your mother says nothing but it is obvious that she doesn't approve. Stretch-marks, pale lightning flashes, descend into your groin.

Your mother sits rustic between us in a print dress. She wears heavy brogue shoes and those thick lisle stockings. When she crosses her legs I can see she is wearing pink bloomers. She has never had a holiday before and finds it difficult to know how to act. She is trying to read the paper but what little breeze there is keeps blowing and turning the pages. Eventually she folds the paper into a small square and reads it like that. She holds the square with one hand and shades her glasses with the other.

Two of the children come running up the beach with that curious quickness they have when they run barefoot over ribbed sand. They are very brown and stark naked, something we know again is disapproved of, by reading their grandmother's silence. They have come for their bucket and spade because they have found a brown ogee thing and they want to bring it and show it to me. The eldest girl, Maeve, runs away becoming incredibly small until she reaches the water's edge. Anne, a year younger, stands beside me with her Kwashiorkor tummy. She has forgotten the brown ogee and is examining something on the rock behind my head. She says 'bloodsuckers' and I turn round. I see one, then look to the side and see another and another. They are all over the rock, minute, pin-point, scarlet spiders.

Maeve comes back with the brown ogee covered with seawater in the bucket. It is a sea-mat and I tell her its name. She contorts and says it is horrible. It is about the size of a child's hand, an elliptical mound covered with spiky hairs. I carry it over to you and you open one eye. I say, 'Look.' Your mother becomes curious and says, 'What is it?' I show it to you, winking with the eye farthest from her but you don't get the allusion because you too ask, 'What is it?' I tell you it is a sea-mat. Maeve goes off waving her spade in the air.

I have disturbed you because you sit up on your towel, gathering your knees up to your chest. I catch your eye and it holds for infinitesimally longer than as if you were just looking. You rise and come over to me and stoop to look in the bucket. I see the whiteness deep between your breasts. Leaning over, your hands on your knees, you raise just your eyes and look at me from between the hanging of your hair. I pretend to talk, watching your mother, who turns away. You squat by the bucket opening your thighs towards me and purse your mouth. You say, 'It is hot,' and smile, then go maddeningly back to lie on your towel.

I reach over into your basket. There is an assortment of children's clothes, your underwear bundled secretly, a squash-bottle, suntan lotion and at last—my jotter and biro. It is a small jotter, the pages held by a wire spiral across the top. I watch you lying in front of me shining with oil. When you lie your breasts almost disappear. There are some hairs peeping at your crotch. Others, lower, have been coyly shaved. On the inside of your right foot is the dark varicose patch which came up after the third baby.

I begin to write what we should, at that minute, be doing. I have never written pornography before and I feel a conspicuous bump appearing in my bathing trunks. I laugh and cross my legs and continue writing. As I come to the end of the second page I have got the couple (with our own names) as far as the hotel room. They begin to strip and caress. I look up and your mother is looking straight at me. She smiles and I smile back at her. She knows I write for a living. I am working. I have just peeled your pants beneath your knees. I proceed to make us do the most fantastical things. My mind is pages ahead of my pen. I can hardly write quickly enough.

At five pages the deed is done and I tear the pages off from the spiral and hand them to you. You turn over and begin to read.

This flurry of movement must have stirred your mother because she comes across to the basket and scrabbles at the bottom for a packet of mints. She sits beside me on the rock, offers me one which I refuse, then pops one into her mouth. For the first time on the holiday she has overcome her shyness to talk to me on her own. She talks of how much she is enjoying herself. The holiday, she says, is taking her out of herself. Her hair is steel-grey darkening at the roots. After your father's death left her on her own we knew that she should get away. I have found her a woman who hides her emotion as much as she can. The most she would allow herself was to tell us how, several times, when she got up in the morning she had put two eggs in the pot. It's the length of the day, she says, that gets her. I knew she was terrified at first in the dining-room but now she is getting used to it and even criticises the slowness of the service. She has struck up an acquaintance with an old priest whom she met in the sitting-room. He walks the beach at low tide, always wearing his hat and carries a rolled pac-a-mac in one hand.

I look at you and you are still reading the pages. You lean on your elbows, your shoulders high and, I see, shaking with laughter. When you are finished you fold the pages smaller and smaller, then turn on your back and close your eyes without so much as a look in our direction.

Your mother decides to go to the water's edge to see the children. She walks with arms folded, unused to having nothing to carry. I go over to you. Without opening your eyes you tell me I am filthy, whispered even though your mother is fifty yards away. You tell me to burn it, tearing it up would not be safe enough. I feel annoyed that you haven't taken it in the spirit in which it was given. I unfold the pages and begin to read it again. The bump reinstates itself. I laugh at some of my artistic attempts—'the chittering noise of the venetian blinds', 'luminous pulsing tide'—I put the pages in my trousers pocket on the rock.

Suddenly Anne comes running. Her mouth is open and screaming. Someone has thrown sand in her face. You sit upright, your voice incredulous that such a thing should happen to your child. Anne, standing, comes to your shoulder. You wrap your arms round her nakedness and call her 'Lamb' and 'Angel' but the child still cries.

You take a tissue from your bag and lick one corner of it and begin to wipe the sticking sand from round her eyes. I watch your face as you do this. Intent, skilful, a beautiful face focused on other-than-me. This, the mother of my children. Your tongue licks out again wetting the tissue. The crying goes on and you begin to scold lightly giving the child enough confidence to stop. 'A big girl like you?' You take the child's cleaned face into the softness of your neck and the tears subside. From the basket miraculously you produce a mint and then you are both away walking, you stooping at the waist to laugh on a level with your child's face.

You stand talking to your mother where the glare of the sand and the sea meet. You are much taller than she. You come back to me covering half the distance in a stiff-legged run. When you reach the rock you point your feet and begin pulling on your jeans. I ask where you are going. You smile at me out of the head hole of your T-shirt, your midriff bare and say that we are going back to the hotel.

'Mammy will be along with the children in an hour or so.'

'What did you tell her?'

'I told her you were dying for a drink before tea.'

We walked quickly back to the hotel. At first we have an arm around each other's waist but it is awkward, like a three-legged race, so we break and just hold hands. In the hotel room there are no venetian blinds but the white net curtains belly and fold in the breeze of the open window. It is hot enough to lie on the coverlet.

It has that special smell by the sea-side and afterwards in the bar as we sit, slaked from the waist down, I tell you so. You smile and we await the return of your mother and our children. ❦

Duncan McLean

COME GO WITH ME

Pellets of hail fell into her hair and settled there. It was hard not to reach out and brush them away. Instead I watched the hail fall on the black of her hair and the red wool of her scarf.

Will we cross? I said.

An artic blundered by. We'll wait for the crossing, she said.

She seemed not to realise her hair was filling up with sleetbeads, though she could've guessed: from out of a dark space above the streetlights it came hailing down all around us, ticking on the slabs of the pavement, crinching under our feet as we walked. We passed a bus shelter and there was a rattling on the metal roof, a pattering of hail on the rubbish in the bin beside it. And all the time it fell silently on her layered black hair, landing first on the surface strands, then, the hair shifting slightly with the movement of her head as she walked, sifting down through the thicknesses. The air was gealcold all about us, and the hailstones didn't melt. I could see them glistening down in the black depths of her hair, small and bright as diamonds.

She slowed. We'd reached the crossing place. She pressed the button and looked out over the road.

Holding my breath, I raised my hand and stroked some of the sleet off her scarf. I didn't touch her hair: I didn't want the heat of my skin to melt the hailstones decked there. She moved her head round slowly to look at me, then smiled.

You're covered in dandruff, she said.

My breath burst out in a laugh, and I shook my head so the hail flew off and tumbled to the ground with the fresh stuff still falling.

You've got it as well, I said. Except it's not dandruff. It's like . . . when my sister got married, and she had this wedding dress with all these layers and layers of white lace cloth, and a veil. And set into the lace were these wee white blobs, that when you looked closer, you saw they were little buds of flowers. All sewn-in hundreds of buds through her wedding dress.

She looked away across the road again. So your sister had a white wedding? She turned her head in the direction of the oncoming traffic. I don't suppose I'd be entitled to one of those. Not after last night.

Eh? Entitled? My sister just fancied it—reckoned she wanted one, entitled or not.

Aye, but . . .

There was a loud beeping behind her.

No buts, I said. There's the green man. She made to step out onto the crossing, but I caught her by the elbow and moved to meet her as she half-turned towards me. No, I said. Green for go. My arms went around her shoulders and we kissed, her hands linking round the small of my back, pressing me in towards her.

We kissed till the beeping stopped, then she moved her head to one side. The green man's flashing, she said.

Bit cold in this weather, surely?

She laughed. I held her and looked all over her face. There were hailstones shining in the fringe of her hair, and a few on the black lashes above her eyes.

Don't move, I said, then leant forward and kissed each eye in turn, lifting the beads of ice off in my lips, feeling them melt immediately on the tip of my tongue. I smiled at her. Frozen tears, I said.

She pulled back, frowned. How did you ken I'd been crying?

What? Crying? I didn't . . .

Oh. Well. She turned aside. Forget it.

You were crying? What about? I was just joking! What were you greeting about?

The green man was going again. She broke away from me and stepped out into the road, half-skiting for a second, then straightening up and striding on. I followed. At the far side she didn't stop, but walked quickly the last few metres to the picture-house. I was right behind her, followed her through the swinging door. She crossed the foyer, went into the bar, and sat down suddenly at one of the small black tables.

I watched as she loosened her scarf, her gaze on the knot. It was forty minutes till the next showing.

I was going to ask about the greeting again, but then I didn't ken how to. What do you want to drink? I said. I knew how to ask that.

She looked up. I'll get them.

It's alright. I shrugged. I'm on my feet and that. Hih! Plus I'm planning to slip you a mickey finn, get you drunk, have my wicked way with you. Again!

Suddenly she brought the end of her scarf up to her eyes and covered them. She held it there for a second, then let it fall and looked up at me, tiny drops of water still hanging on the tips of her eyelashes.

Blinking hailstones, she said, and sniffed.

I stared at her.

After a moment she said, I'll have a mineral water.

Is that all?

Aye.

Are you sure?

She nodded.

When I got back from the bar she'd taken off her coat and was holding it up by the collar, brushing sleet from it with the other hand. I laid the glasses on the table next to the neatly folded scarf.

One whisky with ice, one fizzy water. I sat down.

She stopped brushing the coat, looked at it from top to bottom, then twirled it in her hand and examined the other side. She draped the coat over the stool next to her, and turned to me.

Thanks, she said. She picked up her glass.

So what is it with the water? I said. Too much of the other last night? The other?

Gin.

She smiled, swirled her drink around. No. A lot, but not too much.

I nodded. Me too. Just the right amount.

She looked me in the eye. Yeah. Just right. She held the gaze. I think.

After a second I reached out towards her and put my hand down on the edge of the table, close to where hers was playing with the fringe of the folded-up scarf. The table was giving out wee electric shocks.

Listen, I said. We hardly know each other. I mean we only met about twenty hours ago and, okay, we spent the night together and it was the best night of my life so far—and you said it was good for you too—but basically we don't really know each other, but also basically, I really really like you, ken?

I lifted my hand and laid it on top of hers. That was giving out electric shocks too. She didn't say anything. So I went on.

I mean I really like you and I'd like to get to know you better. But even now, even hardly not knowing you at all, I already . . . care for you. I care for you, and I want to be happy, and here we are sitting here, and you haven't seemed right since we met thenight. You seem to be—well, stop me if I'm being nosey or something here—but you seem to be on the verge of bursting out greeting. I mean I don't ken what I feel exactly, but I ken for sure it's nothing to greet about!

I looked at her. Still she didn't say anything. She pulled her hand out from under mine and reached for her glass. But she didn't raise it to her lips. She just flicked it round so the bubbles whirled into a storm, like birling sleet.

And drinking water, just! I mean, there's nothing wrong with it if that's what you want, but . . . I just get the feeling that something's not right. And I wish you'd tell me what, cause I care, I do care. I care about you.

I waited a long time, but she didn't say anything. The barman put on a tape, turned it up way too loud for a second, then down to quiet. It was fifties doo-wop stuff.

> Dum-dum dum-dum dum
> Doobie doobie
> I love you baby
> Come go with me
> Dum-dum dum-dum dum

I feel a bit sick, she said.

Och . . . I slid my hand across the tabletop so the tips of my fingers were touching the tips of hers. Is that what my company does to you? I said.

She didn't smile, kept looking down. Mind when I made you go away this afternoon? Said I wanted to get a shower and then some messages and that?

Aye. Did you not really?

Aye I did, but I went somewhere else as well. I went to the family planning.

I looked at her.

I went and got one of those morning-after pills, she said. Ken the ones?

Eh . . .

Instant period. Strong stuff. So I've been feeling a bit queasy ever since.

Queasy. Jesus.

She put a hand up to her hair and pushed it back out of her eyes. A spray of hailwater spirked off and dotted down all over the tabletop. I looked at the spirks, thought of sweat on her skin, hail on the pavement, buds shaken free of the wedding lace.

What are you thinking? she said.

Eh . . . I shook my head. Jesus! I looked up at her. I can't believe it, I said. You told me it was okay! I'd never've come inside you if I'd kent it wasn't okay.

She shrugged. It felt okay at the time. A grin. Actually, it felt brilliant.

I picked up my whisky and took a big drink. Aye, I said. But still.

Anyway, she said, it's okay now. Everything's fine. I just feel a bit sick, that's all.

Me too.

Eh?

I finished the whisky and my glass clattered on the table as I put it down.

I get the hint! she said, and dug her wallet out of her coat pocket.

I can't believe it, I said. I'm in shock.

It's true! She stood up. I really am standing my hand!

I raised the tumbler to my lips, but it was empty.

Tell you what, she said. I'll do the drinks and you go for tickets. There'll be crowds appearing soon.

I got up and went ben the foyer. There was a queue at the box office. I stood in it till there was only one person in front of me. Then I stepped out and walked quickly away, through the swinging door, into the street. I started running. I ran back the way we'd just come, dodging across the road before I reached the green man, keeping on fast down the far side, skiting this way and that through the clumps of folk on the pavement.

Dum-dum dum-dum dum.

I stopped. Held breath burst out of my lungs. I leaned back against a lamppost and lifted my face to the white blaze and the cold air. Something stung my cheek. Then my forehead. I blinked. Odd bullets of hail were still coming down from the sky. I closed my eyes and let them hit me. Blood thumped on the drums of my lugs.

Dum-dum dum-dum dum.

After a minute I turned and walked back towards the picture house, my skin numbed with the cold.

I leant my hands on the table. Whisky, no ice, and a gin for her. A hailstone fell from my hair, bounced on the tabletop, and rolled against her scarf.

She looked at it, raised her eyebrows. Sleeting in the foyer, is it?

I picked up my glass and drained the whisky.

It's bloody cold out there! I said.

She nodded. Did you get the tickets?

No, I said, I didn't get the tickets.

Good, she said. Let's go. 🍂

George Friel

AN ANGEL IN HIS HOUSE

She was very much in love with him, but whether her excess of love made her doubt if so much could be returned, or whether she had in fact the intuition ascribed to her sex, she had no faith in his feelings for her. She was only twenty, and her reading was limited to women's weeklies. When she indulged in serious conversation, it went to her head and she staggered round the twin topics of the nature of man and the existence of true love. Like other metaphysicians, she never came to any conclusion about either.

He was one of her schoolgirl idols when she was in the fourth form and he was in the sixth, and it was a great pleasure to her that, when they had both risen to the rank of former pupils, he paid her so much attention at a reunion dance. They went about together for a year after that, and her troubles with him confirmed her tendency to look at life in terms of potted wisdom, as 'You've got to take the rough with the smooth'; 'There's no such thing as real love', and 'Men are brutes'. He had set out on a university course as a medical student, but the change in domestic circumstances after the death of his father forced him to find a job at once and he went to work near the university in a shop that sold medical text-books. He was tall, fair, in boisterous good health, fond of practical jokes, rather coarse, and altogether a knowledgeable young man.

So knowledgeable he alarmed her, and his brashness led her to put an end to their friendship. At least she tried to, but all she meant was that he should put an end to his extreme demands on her and continue more sedately. He chose to see no alternative, and while she sat at home waiting for him to call, thinking he understood and accepted what she meant, he found a nurse in the Western Infirmary to please him. When it became clear that he was not coming back, she wept in bed every night for a month and then wilted a little, getting her compensation for the episode by looking upon herself as a woman wise beyond her years, old before her time, experienced beyond her mother's suspicions.

Before another year was out, she heard from her friends that he was always asking about her, and one of them obligingly gave him the telephone number of her new office. She was not unprepared for his voice when he telephoned her late one autumn afternoon, and yet she had difficulty with her breath and feared he could hear her heart. The conversation was slightly stilted. They were embarrassed, falling into gaps in the uneven terrain of their manoeuvring, then scrambling out with a self-conscious hum and a haw. After five minutes beating about the bush, he put the question to her and she agreed to see him again.

Soon it was as bad as ever, but although she said she had learned her lesson and told him he would never again break her heart by walking out on her because she would keep her heart to herself, all she had in fact learned was she could not do without him. She had just been getting used to it when he telephoned, and not only the depressing dullness of that state, but the long journey she had made to get there, seemed to her equally unthinkable again.

Of course she was often happy with him, simply and untroubledly happy, and there were evenings when he was content to hold her hand in the pictures and no more, and she thought that was wonderful, but it never lasted.

'You know,' she told her confidant in the audit office, Mr. Barlow, 'I'd be perfectly happy just to listen to him talking, just to sit beside him at the fire. But him! He's different.'

It became so bad again that she thought she would have to leave him for good, for her own good. But she was determined that this time he would not leave her under the pretext of failing to see the alternative she offered; she would do the leaving, without any alternative, and frankly and firmly tell him she could not and would not go on. She burst out with it impulsively one evening when he hedged about coming round to her parents two nights later, on New Year's Eve. He knew them already, he had no reason to be shy—her father in particular liked him, but still he hedged. He spoke as if the Scotch custom of a family gathering at Hogmanay was silly, too ridiculous for him to follow.

'You'd think we weren't good enough for you, the way you talk,' she said angrily. 'You're selfish, utterly selfish. You want everything your way, but will you do the least thing for me? No, never! I don't believe you could ever love anybody but yourself. It's the one thing all the time with you. All you do is rush at things, and you never think of anybody else's feelings. The best thing we can do is to stop seeing each other.'

To her dismay he agreed at once. He said, not without a touch of gallantry, that she was too much for him. She would have preferred him to say too good, but he said too much. He could not resist her. It was dangerous to be alone with her, and lately they had managed too many evenings alone. She was quite right; it would be better if they stopped seeing each other.

'Otherwise it can only end in disaster,' he ended remotely.

Only her astonishment kept her from weeping on the spot. She was almost hysterical at the calmness with which he announced he could not be calm in her company, at the complacency with which he took her impulsive suggestion that they should stop meeting. His attitude illuminated for her the insincerity of her proposal, and that, too, was an additional pain. She had thought she was sincere when she mediated it, and she could not understand how it became any the less sincere simply because it found an unguarded expression. She almost shook him as she stood clutching his lapels in their good-night embrace, standing at the porch with him at midnight, the two of them behind the half-closed storm-doors and she with her back to the hall-door.

'It's all very well for you,' she said. 'It's just what I said. You don't care for anybody but yourself. You'd like to pick me up and drop me just whenever it suits you. You could go away tonight and not bother your head if you never saw me again.'

'It was your idea in the first place,' he said stolidly.

In the end they agreed to meet again on New Year's Eve to discuss the proposal that they should not meet again. By habit they made to go to a cinema, but there were queues everywhere, and because it was cold and wet, he said they should go to his mother's house. She had been there before, mildly welcomed by a widow who seemed distracted from matters immediately in front of her and continually casting some unuttered calculation. So she agreed meekly enough; perhaps they would come by half an hour alone while his mother pottered and panned in the kitchen, and they could settle their future in a heart-to-heart talk, or perhaps he would not want to settle it and everything would go on as before. She dimly saw that she didn't know what she wanted, and as they trudged to his mother's house, there was a narrow chasm of silence between them, so easy to cross if she just looked at it rationally, but impossible for her to leap first, and he said nothing.

Then, to her embarrassment, the widow gave her a welcome even more remote than usual; her unfinished calculation seemed more retrospective than ever, and to make her position worse, she was quickly aware that the mother and son were on bad terms. As she waited alone in the front room at a pleasant enough fire, she could hear them in the kitchen carrying on from where they had left off. The mother came through to get a scarf, and without open rudeness ignored her and went back to the kitchen. She heard the son's brusque voice and the mother's sharp reply.

'When you come back from Hilda's,' he was saying.

'If I come back,' snapped the mother.

She heard the front door bang and felt prickly with discomfort.

He came through to her calmly.

'What's wrong?' she asked timidly.

'Oh, nothing,' he said, and kissed her warmly. 'Just one of her moods.'

There was no discussion, no heart-to-heart talk to settle their future. She was always weak when he attacked her, and her muddle about what she wanted made her weaker. He started at once making love to her in the same old way, and she tried for a moment to keep him off with a cold, astonished question.

'How can you? You quarrel with your mother like that, you let her go without even trying to make it up—oh, you're selfish! You think of nobody but yourself. And on New Year's Eve too!'

He slowed down and became all gentle and explanatory. It was a silly little quarrel. It meant nothing. She was often like that. She said things she didn't mean. She would come back as if nothing had happened. She always went round to see Hilda, his married sister, when she was cross with him, and stayed there till bedtime.

'How could I leave you?' he asked fondly. 'You don't want me to leave you, now do you? Tell me the truth.'

The reconciliation he offered was too much for her. He had crossed the narrow chasm of silence, and they stood on the same side, murmuring loving words together, mutually caressing. Within half an hour he had overcome her scruples and had his way. She held out as long as she could, exercising an effort she felt in herself was terrific, but in one last moment, as he persisted, she loosened her grasp and she was beaten and no longer cared.

After it was all over, she wept for ten minutes, and privately wondered what she was fussing about. She was disappointed in herself, that she had done what she had sworn she would never do, and disappointed in what she had done, that it was hardly worth so much curiosity, so much fighting, so much excitement. But he came back to her gratefully, and she took the chance to coax him to come round to her parents after all. He still jibbed at the idea, and she had to break away from him forcibly and threaten to go home alone, to go and get her hat and coat and show she was serious, before he finally agreed to accompany her. The party was warmed up when they arrived, crowded and noisy, for her father was a sociable man. She sat in a corner and drank more than was good for her, and when her seducer stood up to leave the party he had never wanted to attend, she startled the company by mouthing drunkenly, 'Don't let him go! Don't let him go! If he goes away, I'll never see him again.'

She began to cry, talking away to herself indistinctly, and every-body asked everybody else who had given her all the drink. But since it was Hogmanay and nobody was quite sober, her condition was looked upon as amusing rather than serious, the more so since young love was always a topic for a joke.

She was back at work on the second day of the New Year and felt an urge to confide in Mr. Barlow again. She had to wait till after lunch to get him alone, and slipped away from the canteen back to her seat in the typing pool with her knitting. Mr. Barlow sat in the farthest corner. He never went to the canteen, but lunched at his supervisor's table from a flask that contained something that wasn't tea, and a package of rye bread. There was supposed to be something wrong with his stomach. He was middle-aged, or looked it, and if he was married, widowed, divorced or single, nobody knew. He listened but said little. Perhaps that was why she had got into the habit of returning early from her lunch to chat with him alone. She could never have said if she even as much as liked him; he was beyond liking or disliking. But he had always kept her secrets, and the little he said made her feel friendly. He was like a wall that looks adequate, not a splendid piece of architecture, but the right height to lean on.

She parked her knitting and her bag, took off her coat and strolled up to him.

'Hello, Helen,' he said, putting his flask away and screwing up the paper bag that had carried his sandwiches. No one ever actually saw him eat, but it was assumed he did so since he was apparently still alive.

She sat down across the table from him and plunged into the heart of it.

'It's all over, finished, *zu Ende*,' she said. Having once found he understood her fifth-form German, she occasionally used to him such phrases as she could remember.

He looked at her deeply and waited.

She told him all she could as openly as she could, getting round the difficulty of directly telling him she had lost her chastity by saying, 'So when his mother went out we were all alone till near on midnight, and you can think what you like.'

Whatever he thought, he said nothing. She blurted on.

'Well, anyway, I know what I'm missing now. And it's not worth all that much.'

'I agree,' he said. 'But it's a pity you had to find it out that way.'

She took a cigarette from him sadly and he looked at her curiously as he lit it. She had good looks but no beauty, a strong body and a wilful mouth.

'But why are you so sure it's all over?' he asked. 'All that talk of ending it was before you—'

He stopped and left it without words.

'I know,' she said. 'But—oh, I don't know. I don't know what's in his mind.'

Because they seemed to encourage her a little, he repeated some commonplace words of comfort he did not believe, and out of simple kind-heartedness, he elaborated his platitudes, looking at her eyes and marvelling at the burden women took upon themselves in the name of love. She sat staring into the future, and he saw she was at once frightened and allured by the threat of motherhood. The worry in her eyes faded as he chattered on, speaking to her at length for once, and he was amazed to see it go so quickly. He was certain that even if her conqueror did telephone her during the week, he would not take long after that to arrange his exit; or if he ever did marry her, which he could not believe, then indeed

> No sweet aspersions would the heavens let fall
> To make that contract grow, but barren hate,
> Sour-eyed disdain and discord would bestrew
> The union of their bed with weeds so loathly
> That they would hate it both . . .

But instead of saying so, he said gently, making the sentimentality palatable with an ironic smile. 'No, don't you worry. You'll be all right. I'll live to see you engaged at the summer and married at Christmas. And you'll be a loving, attentive wife, an angel in the house, and you'll send him out with his trousers pressed, and you'll polish his shoes for him and—'

'Oh no,' she interrupted him quickly. 'Oh no! That's one thing I'll never do. I can't imagine anything more servile. There are some things I wouldn't do for any man, and polishing his shoes is one of them.' ❦

Gordon Legge

I NEVER THOUGHT IT WOULD BE YOU

Sharon gets merry and talks gibberish when she's stoned. Me, I just get mellow and sluggish. So I wasn't really giving her what you'd call my undivided attention until she kissed me on the cheek and said, 'I never thought it would be you, that's for sure.' I asked what she was on about but she just said, 'You know' like it was a question or something. From the glint in her eye, I suspect she was talking about us.

We scored our dope earlier on round at Colin's. Sharon doesn't like Colin or that lot—and they don't like her. She's a funny person, not a fun person, kind of privately witty as opposed to the more publicly wanton (i.e. thick) types they go for. Anyway, Colin had a crowd of them in and my attention was drawn to a rather plump girl taking in a massive blast from Colin's hookah pipe. (Identical to the one in *Raiders of the Lost Ark*, Colin never tires of telling folk.) She was well gone and didn't recognize me or my name. I recognized her, though, and could put a name to her, no problem. You see the girl in question was my first-ever proper girlfriend. My childhood sweetheart. She was there with some English guy from over the old town she now lives with. To be honest, she looked a bit silly. She had on those really tight ski-pants (which she had to keep pulling up), high heels and a baggy, hooped top which kept sliding down to reveal her flesh-coloured bra-straps. Like a lot of the women round here she was wee, fat and dumpy with that short, uninteresting hair more suited to the older generation.

It was pointless us staying since they were all so out of it, so basically we just said, 'Hello/How you doing?/See you soon/Cheerio'. Sharon wouldn't go within a mile of that pipe, anyway.

On our way home, Sharon said the girl on the pipe could have been quite pretty if she'd learn how to put her lips together right. Sharon says things like that. She picks out flaws in people and renames them accordingly. My childhood sweetheart is now immortalized as squintlips.

This is my longest relationship and only the first time I've lived with someone. I was engaged when I was seventeen but—to tell the truth—it was something you did when you were that age; like taking driving lessons or visiting lots of different pubs. All these previous relationships ended with me storming off. I made out that I just wanted to party all the time but that wasn't the truth. It would be truer to say I never felt I was being shown enough affection. I was always anxious for company but once I'd secured it, it never seemed to satisfy. The chase had been more satisfying. When I said 'I love you' I was begging a response. It's different now. No, *I'm* different now. Before, I'd have gone off and shagged someone else and that would have been the end of it. Not now. For once I've seen something through. I've stuck with something and I like what it's become. Those three little words are now said with a smile. Like laughter, they express a reaction. I'm comfortable with that distance that sometimes comes between us. I'm comfortable with silence, too. Never used to be. But then I used to be terrified of spiders.

We've both lived here all our lives and we'd known each other for years before we got together. I guess that's what she meant by 'I never thought it would be you'. She was the trophy and I was the winner.

Life with my childhood sweetheart was somewhat different, and, in retrospect, somewhat prophetic. She stayed over the back and we got each other to and from school, spent the evenings together then sent coded messages at bedtime using the venetian blinds. We were in and out of each other's houses all the time, just coming and going as we pleased. I got treated like her brother when I went there. That means I got crisps and helped myself to juice. It also means I got rows and had to help with the washing-up.

On Saturday mornings we went to the old ice-rink. My skates doubled as weapons, ready to slash anybody that acted out of turn. I used to spend hours in front of the mirror, fantasizing about protecting old squintlips. She was the one who told me that if she stuck her tongue in my mouth I'd get a hard-on. A point I took great pleasure in her proving. We split up soon afterwards cause she wouldn't let me shag her. (That's the prophetic bit.)

I started hanging about with my brothers and their mates. They were older and they smoked and played some fairly serious games of football on the school pitch at night. Following one of these games I got to shag one of our groupies, Lynn 'Bucket' Sommerville, in the kiddies pipe round the back of Connery Place on a night when the rain just pissed down. I wasn't the first person to have done this—but if she kept records I was probably the quickest. I should have been more patient with old squintlips.

Me and Sharon have had a few problems recently. Most of them come from me: my friends and my family. They're not friends really, just guys from work I go out to get rubbered with. Guys whose wives are called 'her' and who spend their time and wages in pubs. Going out for a drink with them means you get well blottoed and you spend a fair bit of money. The other night me and Sharon had a verbal set-to on account of me blowing forty quid in an afternoon drinking session. I tried to explain that sometimes I have this incredible desire just to forget about everything and get absolutely wrecked. (This comes about the sixth pint. The pint of no return. Sorry.) I'm slow to think and clumsy when I talk so this came out sounding like me saying that the money that went on the house was her money and that I was entitled to the occasional afternoon out. I say some pretty stupid things when I argue with Sharon. I always end up sounding holier than thou. The trouble is I like getting pissed. I feel I talk a lot of sense when I'm pissed. There's this Chinese boy I know who talks perfect English after six pints of Guinness, that's kind of the way I see myself. I know it wouldn't be the end of the world if I gave up those afternoon sessions with the boys from work—I mean, forty quid—and I know it's all acting, hamming it up with the lads, but I like that. I've always done it. I thought I always would.

Sometimes I take this home with me and I'll go, 'The trouble with you is . . . It's about time you . . . you . . . you . . . you . . . '. Sharon swallows and says, 'Okay then.' Then she pretends to go off in the huff. There is no such thing as Sharon letting me win an argument. What she's doing is biding her time, cause you can bet your bottom dollar that she'll come back with one of her perfect, sarky comments. As I said, she's funny, not fun, she's also a piss-taker rather than a ball-breaker. She knows I'll open my mouth and make a complete cunt of myself. Her favourite put-down is to remind me that I have no sense of smell. It works as sarcasm and it hurts.

Our families don't help. That's her sisters and my brothers: her Diane and her Peggy and my Andrew and my Martin. Her sisters are doing well—my brothers should be doing time. She visits her lot and goes shopping—my lot come round to cadge fags and money. They've stolen from her. Stole twenty quid once. They pleaded their innocence, of course, knowing that I would stick up for them. Brother that I am, I duly did. But when things returned to normal I took them aside and told them if it ever happened again I would take their noses off. I was quite proud of myself. I meant it. My brothers can be tiresome. They go on about the trouble they've been in and the women they've been seeing. This leads them onto stories from the past involving me. Sharon doesn't bother about these stories. She's got a broad back and dismisses my brothers in terms of smell—Andrew of ammonia and Martin of methane. They don't get it. My brothers used to come away with stories concerning Sharon. Who she'd been out with and what happened, that kind of thing. At first they bothered me but not anymore. I'm glad there were others before me. Maybe that's what she meant by 'I never thought it would be you'. She was the booby prize and I was the lumber.

Sharon's sisters don't care much for me. One of them told me as much when she said all men treated all women like shit. Like, you're excused, you can't help being a man. Actually, her sisters and me get on all right. It's friendly banter mostly. They're really protective of her. She's the baby of the family. She doesn't tell them she smokes dope, although I suspect they know. They're not stupid.

I don't know whether that's true about all men treating all women like shit. I'm trying to think of examples that contradict and I'm struggling. My dad? No. My friends? Mmmmm some. Only some. Guys from work? No. My brothers? Case proved. Me? . . . No, until recently. Yeah, until Sharon. She'd disagree. She'd laugh at that. What generalizations can you make about women? Moody.

I like her when she's like this. Normally she doesn't fit in too well with my world. Like in pubs or at gigs she gets bored quickly and invents a headache so we have to leave. I'm not bothered. If she's not happy we're as well not being there. And as for getting her to come and watch me playing in the summer league—eh, that's a non-starter. But she likes her wee bit of blow does Sharon.

I encourage her to smoke dope because all the couples I know that smoke together stay together. They have stable, long-term relationships. They function as a team. You think of them in those terms. Maybe it's just the people I know, but that's the way I see things. That's what I aspire to.

If that sounds a bit desperate then maybe I am. Sharon's taken to this and I'll go along with it. I don't get the same hit as her, though, I'm not relaxed, I'm agitated. Anyway, that's my problem. It's not something we talk about.

The best nights out we have (and, I believe, the best nights out anybody could have) are when we take our wee bit of dope round to Keith's and Ruth's. We try to time our visits to coincide with those of Eddie and Jane. Keith and Eddie are brilliant when they get going. They tell their stories from when they used to have the band, and they had their mild flirtation with fame. It's the same stories every time we see them but what the hell. Sharon loves those nights out. She laughs till she's sore.

Sharon said, 'I never thought it would be you.' I was thinking I couldn't say that because it's too glib. There's a whiff of disappointment in there as well. Women are like that. They specialize in rabbiting on for hours about nothing in particular, then out of the blue comes something that does your head in. It keeps you on your toes.

But, as I'm sure she would point out, I'm clumsy and I don't have a sense of smell. I forgot she kissed me when she said it. No, I didn't forget. It's just that that wasn't where I'd put the emphasis. Actions speak louder than words. That's one of hers. Especially when I'm drunk. It's worth thinking about. It's worth remembering. ❦

Neil M. Gunn

THE OLD MAN

He was the Old Man of the gipsy tribe, and his work consisted entirely in settling the disputes of the upcoming generations. Any evening—or morning, for that matter—he could be found sitting on a dry log smoking his pipe and looking meditatively and pleasantly at whatever was or was not before him.

His advice was most frequently sought after a Saturday's night bout of methylated-spirit drinking, mixed fights and a night or two in the cells. His dispensing of justice followed the invariable practice of never inflicting any penalty beyond his own speech. And his speech rarely began until they had talked themselves hoarse and sometimes into a fight on the spot.

But when he began speaking, he kept going. No mere verbal interruption, however explosive, stopped him. And he talked 'like a book'. It was even said that he had read old books in his young days, just because he was descended from a ditchside poet in the year one. More than once opposing sides had combined to call him a windbag and other uncomplimentary terms, and had retired, in new-found harmony, shouting at him as he still went on talking. But such derision would be short-lived. Presently they would splutter and laugh among themselves and say, 'Did anyone ever hear such an ould fool?' If the money could run to it, they would bring him a sup of whisky, or a finger of black twist tobacco. For long enough the camp would be a scene of harmonious endeavour, bounded on the right side by horse-dealing and on the left by begging.

However, every now and then he had to arbitrate on difficult matters. A single person would come with a deep personal grievance, touching theft, or hatred. It was not always easy. As each and all came voluntarily, they felt entitled to the advice or backing they specially desired.

But sometimes a man came when his mind was a dark whirl, and then he would not put his point, but talk round about it or remain gloomily silent. This was the most difficult case of all. It gave the Old Man scope. Dan's was a case of this sort.

The snout of his cap well down over his left eye, Dan looked gloomy and raven-dark. His petulant mouth, too, was bitter. When he spat explosively, he turned his nose away at once from the spit as from his own thought or the other fellow's argument. He had white teeth, a brown rich skin, and was just turned thirty. In the way he would often not look at you there was something of a spoilt boy or a warped criminal.

The Old Man said nothing.

In the silence, Dan wriggled and kicked the rotten end of the log, not hard, but persistently.

'I feel every kick in me,' said the Old Man at last.

'Ye won't feel it much longer,' said Dan. 'I'm for off.'

'Indeed,' said the Old Man politely. 'Are you going soon?'

'I'm going at once,' said Dan savagely, and he stopped kicking and looked away.

'If you have now finished what you are going to say and want my opinion on it, I'll give it to you.'

'What d'ye think ye're talking about?' asked Dan with brutal sarcasm.

'It's a very difficult situation,' nodded the Old Man, 'very difficult. But it has this to it that it's not new. Accordingly, I can make a few remarks on it in a general way to begin with, for I have found that nearly every trouble in life lifts like a mist once the understanding understands and shines into it.'

'Horn spoons!' said Dan.

'Take a case, for example, of a man and his wife. They fall out.'

'Who fell out?'

'They fall out more than once. Until the time comes when they are in a continuous state of having fallen out. It is one of the queerest states in the world, that, and one of the most critical. Now the word critical has two meanings. For instance, take the rotten old swing-bridge down there before it broke under you last week. When you were on the middle of it, it was in a critical condition, and—listen, now—you were critical of it being in that critical condition.'

'Are you trying to make a fool of me, or what?' asked Dan threateningly.

'So it is with marriage. The two supports of the bridge, as you would say, are in a critical condition, and so are critical one to another. The female support or wife will become critical of the male support or husband. As he moves about in his bad nature, she will see all the nasty things in him that she missed before. She will see first of all that he is ill-tempered, and then she will see that he is mean-spirited, and then she will see that he notices little things like any miser, and then she will see that he is a bully, and finally she will see that he is cruel. Everything, in fact, that she thought he hadn't got, she now sees that he has got. She thought him always a good cut above other men, now she sees that he is below them, for they are manly to their wives whatever else. When she grows ashamed of him in company—'

'What the blazes—'

'Hsh,' said the Old Man. 'There's your wife coming round the quarry.'

At that, Dan's expression grew so vindictive that it was clear he would gladly have smitten the Old Man out of existence if he could have done it in time. He spat, stubbornly held his ground, and did not look round. When next he gathered sense in the Old Man's words, they were flowing: '. . . so he becomes critical of her. He had thought her a good-looker, and he wonders to himself bitterly where his eyes could have been. He had thought she had spirit and was full of fun, and now she goes about more silent than a funeral, with an expression of misery that if you could get it in a bottle would do for rennet. He bawls at her and she does not answer, and that is enough to drive a lively man to murder. And then she will say something that is worse than saying nothing. When he cannot eat from anger the small noises she will be making eating steadily like a blind cow will make him want to vomit, and then he gets up and kicks the bottom out of the stool he was sitting on.'

'Who the hell told you I kicked the bottom—'

'Then he begins to notice . . .'

'Will ye listen to me?'

'. . . little things that he would be ashamed to tell anyone he noticed. But I can explain that better if, first of all, I compare this wife of his with a young woman he saw singing a ballad song at the horse fair at Knockfalish. The sound of her voice would draw the heart out of you, and she had a shy dark eye more impudent than a bad woman's kiss. When you would be standing there looking at her, you would think to yourself that the whole world could roar to hell in the glory of a dozen or maybe thirteen fights, if—'

'Will ye stop yer gab?' roared Dan, and he caught the Old Man by the whiskers.

'Well,' said the Old Man calmly, 'have you thought of your complaint yet?'

'Complaint!' When Dan got back his breath he laughed—and roared, 'Has my wife been talking to you?'

'No. She is the kind who would never talk to me.'

Dan glared at him and threw his whiskers aside. 'Begod, ye're right there. What the hell then have ye been talking about?'

'I have just been filling in time till you could put words on your complaint. And surely the relations between a man and a woman are interesting at any time. For the first time in six months my egg was boiled hard as a stone this morning, and I can only take it soft.'

Dan gave a roar of laughter, and took off his bonnet and put it on again. 'You, who haven't done a stroke of work in twenty years! You, whose wife has never stopped working for ye in twenty years! You're the one to know about marriage!'

'Well, don't you think I am?' asked the Old Man.

'Ye ould hairy amadan, you!' cried Dan, swaying on his feet. 'This is as good as a fair!'

'As I was saying—'

'Oh, shut yer mouth,' said Dan, 'and tell me this.' And when he had stopped the Old Man, he bellowed derisively, 'D'ye mean to tell me that is the way of it between people and them married?'

'That is the way,' said the Old Man.

'Between all people?'

'Between all people, everywhere, high and low. To every married couple, from the king and the queen on their thrones to the.

horse-dealers at Knockfalish Fair, a time comes when that is the way, for better or for worse, for longer or for shorter.'

'And who told ye about the kings and queens? Eh?'

'In the old histories of our country . . .'

'Stop now, will you? Stop!'

'. . . the ancient kings and queens would be quarrelling in a way that was known to every story-teller that slept in a ditch. Moreover they—'

'I believe ye there,' said Dan. 'I've heard the stories myself.' He marvelled for a short time, his eyes in a bright humour; then he forcibly stopped the Old Man once more.

'Tell me this,' he said, looking at him narrowly, so that he should not escape him. 'Tell me this. How d'ye know the exact things they would be thinking of one another? Tell me, now. Come on!'

'How should I know but out of the wide experience I have gained from life? Do you think when I am sitting here alone that I am doing nothing at all? Is it for the like of you—'

But Dan got him stopped by shouting into his ear, 'If it is the same with everyone, then it must have been the same with yourself?'

'Manifestly,' said the Old Man.

At which great word, Dan roared afresh and tweaked the grey beard in sport. 'Are ye telling me!' he cried.

The Old Man smoothed his beard calmly. 'I don't like anyone,' he said coldly, 'to touch my whiskers.'

Whereat Dan doubled up.

The Old Man remained silent.

'Is it offended ye are now?' asked Dan, pausing in his laughter to enjoy this new delight.

But presently he said coaxingly, 'Ach, now, what are ye offended about? Aren't ye the wisest man in the world? Don't we all know it? Come, now, don't ye be offended with me. I'm going away off to the town this night and bedamn if I won't take back as nice a drop in the heel of a flask for you as ever you tasted. Only, tell me this

now, and it's all I'll ask. Tell me.' His voice lowered confidentially.
'When ye were in that state with herself—how did ye get out of it?
Wait! One minute! First of all, was the state ye were in with one
another as bad as you have made it out to be? And look!' added Dan
threateningly. 'If ye tell me a lie I swear on my soul I'll pull the
whiskers clean out of you.'

'It was worse,' said the Old Man calmly. 'Much worse.'

'Good,' said Dan. 'Go on.'

'It was the end. The only thing that was worse than seeing her in
my sight was thinking of her out of my sight. And every time I had
a look at her out of the corner of my eye, I saw something that made
me worse than ever. Sometimes it would be no more than a drop to
her nose, or hair sticking out over her ear, or lines in her neck, or a
bunch in her clothes, but each small thing would be the last hay
seed. Do you know, when I would be going back to her sometimes
there would be a reluctance on me like a sick pain. And the way that
would make me stop and use words enough to commit my soul, and
I would smash my heels in the ground and walk round myself in a
small circle . . .'

'Whist!' said Dan, taking a turn round about himself. 'That will do
for that.' He was lost in wonder for a minute and then gave a small
chuckle.

'. . . so there we were in the wood . . .'

'What wood was that?' asked Dan. 'Begin that bit again, will you?'

'. . . and the words spoken. I walked away from her. She said
nothing. She did not ask me to stay. She did not plead. It was all
over. It was finished. Before you can say words of parting like that
you have to work yourself into a great rage. I had worked myself so
high that a fear got hold of me that she might do harm to herself.
For it is never the women who threaten to take their own lives who
do take them. It's always the quiet women who have never said
cheep.'

'Are ye telling me that?'

'Yes. You watch them, Dan. Watch the quiet women.'

'Go on,' said Dan thoughtfully.

'It may be difficult for me to get you to understand, for in that wood a queer thing happened to me. Thinking, as I told you, that she might do harm to herself, I stopped in my tracks, and turned, and went back quietly to the wood. I stole from tree to tree until at last I saw her again, all alone by herself, in that quiet place, with the trees like gallows, where she could do to herself what she might be in the mind to do and no one to say her no.'

'And what was she doing?' asked Dan.

'She was gathering sticks,' said the Old Man.

'Gathering . . .' A gust of laughter choked the words in his mouth. Twice he looked at the solemn Old Man and twice he laughed. Then he asked, 'What did ye do?'

'I sat down and watched her. She went slowly from tree to tree gathering the sticks. She broke them, as she gathered them, into lengths, and made a heap of them. And it was while she was doing this with no one to see her in that lonely wood but my own eyes—it was while she was doing this that the true vision of her came to me. I saw her like the mother of generations, the gatherer and the provider; and I thought to myself that this is the greatness of great women, that this is what remains when all the tempers and vanities of great fools of men have passed on the wind.'

'Did ye now? God, and weren't you the great ass! You'll be telling me you wept next.'

'I wept,' said the Old Man.

'Jehosaphat!' said Dan, and his breath went from him. It came back in a gulp of derision at this old fool of a woman before him. 'And to think that we would be wasting time on getting advice from the like of that!'

But the Old Man protected his beard with a smoothing hand. 'Time is never wasted,' said he.

'Isn't it now? And what advice d'ye think you have been giving me?'

'If I haven't been giving you advice,' said the Old Man, 'I have been giving your wife time.'

'What's that ye say? Giving her time for what?'

'When she passed out by a little while ago, going towards the Quiet Wood, I noticed that she had a rope hidden on her. I noticed it because of an end which hung in sight with a loop on it.'

'What . . .'

'What would she be wanting with a rope and a tree and her married to a man like you? It's very difficult for me to answer you that, Dan, but, as I told you before, she is a quiet woman.'

Dan swole up with the wrath that was in him, and drew back his fist to clout the Old Man a blow that would finish him. But the other fist, intending to push the Old Man straight, tipped him heels up over the log. After Dan had said a few words, he began to hurry towards the Quiet Wood.

He was in time, thank God! for she had not yet got the rope fixed. From behind the trunk of a tree he watched her, and had great trouble to keep himself from laughing, for she had tied a small stone to one end of the rope and was trying to throw the stone up over a branch; and not only that, but as any fool could see, the branch was rotten!

The shapes she made at throwing the stone convulsed him, for he could have shot it from his thumb-nail; but she was persistent, never losing her temper; she was like doom; and when, at the fourth throw, she got it over, Dan stopped laughing. She lowered the stone towards her. She's got it now! he thought. But she was in no hurry. She took her breath for a little, standing quite still; then she stirred and looked up at the branch. Would it be strong enough? She tried it; she tugged at it; she tested it with her full weight from a little jump. Crack! and the branch, snapping, fell on top of her fallen body.

Dan fell too and stuffed his mouth. The fun of it was too much for him. And when she sat up and began rubbing her head like a clown in a circus, he turned on his belly, rooting in the friendly earth. 'Are ye seein' her?' he asked the earth. 'Whist! for God's sake!'

When he looked again she was on her feet, dragging the branch over to a big stone. And then he perceived the reason and purpose of all her acts. She was not hanging herself at all: she was gathering sticks!

He was speechless for a long time, seeing only what a fool he had been, what an ass. The ass swole up and went stalking through all the air to heaven. He clenched his fists in wrath, he began to laugh at himself in derision, in unholy mirth, and then just to laugh inwardly.

At last she had so great a bundle tied round with the rope that she couldn't lift it to her back. He watched her like a man with a bet on a horse, but she couldn't do it.

'Blast ye!' he said, for his mind had put his money on her.

But was she beaten? She dragged the pile to the top of a little bank and got below it. Straining heavily at the neck, she heaved upward, steadied herself and her bundle for a moment, then, bent double, began to stagger away. The end of a stick, jutting from the bundle, grazed a tree and swung her round, and the bundle fell. She looked at it dumbly, then began dragging it back to the little bank.

The sight of her doing this was more than flesh and blood could stand. He jumped up and strode down upon her. 'What in the name of little frogs are ye thinking ye're trying to do? Is it ye have lost yer senses entirely? If the thing was too heavy for you, couldn't ye take a stick or two out?'

Her young face looked grey and ancient. There was a dumb misery upon her like the weight of all the world.

'Can't you speak?' he shouted.

'I am tired, Dan,' she said. The last shred of fight had gone from her voice. It sounded small and thin, and haunting as a child's.

'Mother of God.' he cried harshly and pulled her against him so that she might not see whatever happened to his eyes, for a wild gush of feeling had started up behind them. ❦

Ali Smith

THE WORLD WITH LOVE

O n a day when it looks like rain and you're wandering between stations in a city you don't know very well, you meet a woman in the street whom you haven't seen for fifteen years, not since you were at school. She has three children with her, one of them is even quite old, nearly the age you were when you were both friends, a girl who looks so like her mother did then that you shake your heads at each other and laugh. You tell each other how well you both look, she asks you about your job, you ask her about her children, she tells you she's just bought a sweatshirt with the name of the city on it for her daughter (they're visiting for the day) but she's refusing to wear it and it cost nearly twenty pounds. Her daughter, thin and determined-looking, glares at you as if daring you to make any comment at all. She reminds you so much of the girl you knew that your head fills with the time she smashed someone's guitar by throwing it out of the art room window, and you remember she had a dog called Rex. You decide not to mention the guitar and ask after the dog instead. He died ten years ago, she tells you. Then neither of you is quite sure what to say next. You're about to say goodbye when she says to you out of the blue, God Sam, do you remember that time the Ark went mad?

For a moment you don't know what she's talking about and you picture the animals baying and barking, snarling at each other and at the different species round them, at fat Noah and his family trying to keep the noise down. Then it comes, of course it comes, God yes, you say, what a day, eh? and as you're walking along the road, late for your appointment, it all comes, it all comes flooding back.

The French teacher, the Ark everybody called her because her name was Mrs Flood. She liked you, she liked you especially, you were clever. She liked you so much that you hated her class, you hated it when she asked you, and she always did with that tone in her voice that meant, you won't disappoint me, you'll give me the answer, you'll know what it means, you'll know how to say it. The day she called you Sam instead of your full name in front of all your friends, like she was your friend or something, you were mortified, how dare she? How dare she single you out, how dare she make you seem clever in front of everybody? Eventually you began to slip a few wrong answers in, and when you did the other girls had no excuse to give you a hard time afterwards.

Mrs Flood always talking about the beauty of French literature with her singsongy highland island voice, scared of the tough mainland boys and the tough mainland girls, scared of your class even though you were the top stream, not much older than you herself really, her hair rolled up round her ears like the princess in

Star Wars, her eyes like a shy rabbit, her plastic bangles on her wrist jangling into each other as she wrote beautiful French across the board in round letters, *Echo, parlant quant bruit on maine, Dessus rivière ou sus estan, Qui beauté eut trop plus qu'humaine*, pointing to the verbs with the pointer, *j'aurais voulu pleurer* she wrote, *mais je sentais mon coeur plus aride que le désert*, Sam, can you tell me the names for the tenses? she pleaded, and Sally Stewart's friend Donna poked you in the back and jeered in your ear, so it's *Sam* now is it, it's *Sam* now.

Do you remember the time the Ark went mad? The day you came into the classroom and sat down and got your books out as usual and she was standing at the window, staring out over the playing-fields, ignoring the noise level rising behind her as minute after minute passed, ten, fifteen, and each of you realising that it was as if she didn't even know you were there, she wasn't going to turn round, there wasn't going to be any French today. This was the day that one of the boys had brought in a ball of string and the people in the back rows began to tie all the desks at the back together, a network of string woven between the passageways. Somebody coughed out loud, then someone else made a rude noise and you all laughed in relief, but the Ark didn't move, didn't seem to hear. Then Sally Stewart crept out front and stood there like the teacher, you were all giggling, snorting with laughter, and still the Ark didn't turn round and Sally got braver and braver, touching, moving things around on the teacher's table.

She opened the big black dictionary in the middle, letting the cover hit the table with a crash. The Ark didn't look round, she didn't move, not even then, and Sally Stewart was flicking through it and then she was writing on the board the words *le penis*, then *le testicule, les organes genitaux*, she got bolder, and in a teacher voice she said, I'm taking the class today since Mrs Flood isn't here. Who knows the word for to have it off? Who knows the word for french letters?

The boys were roaring, whistling, shouting, the girls were hissing high-pitched laughs, someone, you can't remember who, pulled the poster of the Eiffel Tower off the wall and it got passed round the class. You were laughing and laughing in that scared way and then you noticed that the new girl Laura Watt in front of you three along wasn't laughing, not at all, she was watching, her eyes were going back and fore from Sally at the board to the woman at the window, the Ark, the shoulderblades in her cardigan, her hands resting on the window-sill and her eyes watching a seagull gliding from the roof of the huts to the field. Laura Watt, the new girl, watching it all from behind her dark straight fringe, her chin on her hand, leaning on her elbow watching it. The girl who even though you hardly knew her had heard you say you liked a song and had made you a tape of the whole album, Kate Bush, *The Kick Inside*, and copied out all the songwords off the back of the sleeve for you in her nice handwriting, even though you hardly knew her, had hardly spoken to her. The paper with the words on it folded inside the tape box smelt strange, different, of what it must be like to be in her house or maybe her room, it was a scent you didn't want to lose so you found you were only letting yourself fold the pages open when you really needed to know what the songwords were.

Then Mrs Flood turned round and everything went quiet. Sally Stewart froze at the table with her hand on the dictionary, it was Sally Stewart who looked scared now, not Mrs Flood, who was laughing in a croaky way at the words on the board and who came across, cuffed Sally quite gently on the back of the head and gave her a push back to her seat.

Mrs Flood rolled the blackboard up and she read again what Sally had written on it. She added some accents to some e's, she put a chalk line through *les lettres francaises* and wrote above, the word *preservatif*. Then she pushed the board right up and wrote in large letters, bangles jangling in the silence, the words Look Upon The World With Love. Then she sat down at the table.

Write that down, she said, write it all down. Heads bent, you wrote it in your jotters, the words look upon the world with love, then you looked around at each other, and you carried on writing down the words on the board, the sex words Sally had found in the dictionary. You were writing until all of a sudden the Ark slammed the dictionary shut and said firmly, now, get out. Go on, she said when nobody moved, go on, off you go, get out, and slowly, unsurely, you all packed your books up and went, the people at the back had to pick their way through the webs of string tied between the desks, and it wasn't until you were out in the corridor that you opened your eyes wide at your friends around you and you all made faces at each other as if to say God! and it wasn't until you were on the turn of the stairs that you let yourself say out loud God! what was all that about? and laughter broke out, and the whole class was clattering madly down the stairs, so noisy that the secretary came out of the headmaster's office to see what was happening and the class was rounded up and made to sit on the floor in the hall until it was time for the next period, and several of your friends were personally interviewed about it by the headmaster though you weren't. Mrs Flood was off school for three months and when she came back you didn't have her any more though you always smiled hello at her in the corridor even though she was obviously a weirdo. And remembering it all like this you can't help but remember what you had really forgotten, dark Laura Watt, and how once you even followed her home from school, keeping at a safe invisible distance on your racer, you watched her come to a house and go up a path and look in her pockets for a key and open the door and shut it behind her, you stood outside her house behind a hedge across the road for half an hour then you cycled home again, your heart in your throat.

Laura Watt, you had found you were thinking about her a lot. You scared yourself with how much you were thinking about her, and with how you were thinking about her. You thought of her with words that gave you an unnameable feeling at the bottom of your spine and deep in your guts. Because you couldn't even say them to yourself, you wrote lists of them in a notebook and you kept the notebook inside the Cluedo box under your bed. In case anyone were to find it you wrote the words FRENCH VOCABULARY on the cover and you filled it with words for the hands, the arms, the shoulders, the neck, the mouth. Words for the lips, the tongue, the fingers, the eyes, the eyes brown, the hair dark, the horse dark (a joke). Words you could only imagine, words like caresses, *les cuisses*. That word was enough to thrill you for three whole days, staring into space over your supper, your mother irritated, asking you what was the matter with you, you saying angrily, there is nothing at all the matter with me, your father and mother exchanging glances and being especially nice to you all that evening.

At night when everybody else was asleep you went through your pocket dictionary page by page from a to z and wrote in your notebook every word that might be relevant. *L'amie, l'amour, l'anarchie, l'anatomie, l'ange, être aux anges, anticiper.* Your French marks went up even higher, the new teacher, a nice Glaswegian girl who looked a bit like Nana Mouskouri, told you on the quiet (she understood these things) that you were the only person in the class who knew how to use the subjunctive. If it were to happen, she wrote on the board. You all copied it down, you watched the heads bent, the head bent three along and in front, you all copied down the words. If I were to say. If you were to see.

In the end you got the highest mark in the class and the only A for the exam in the whole school, you got the fifth year prize and you chose a copy of D H Lawrence's *The Virgin and the Gypsy* because it had naked people on the front and you and your friends thought it would be funny to see the Provost's face when he had to present you with it on prizegiving night. But on the night of the ceremony the Provost was a bit drunk, he mixed up the pages of his speech and he muddled the order of the prizes, when it was your turn to go up on stage with everybody clapping he gave you a book called

Sailing Small Yachts and afterwards you had to go round like everybody else trying to find the right book and the owner of the book you'd been given.

Laura Watt was playing the violin at the prizegiving, she was top in music and was going to study it at university. One of the music teachers accompanied her on the piano and she played something by Mozart, you couldn't believe the quickness and slyness of her fingers on the strings and the way the music went through you like electricity, she was really good, everybody clapped, you clapped as loud as you could, you wanted to tell her afterwards, that was really great, you went up to her and she showed you the book the Provost had given her, it was *The Observer Book of Tropical Fish*. I don't have any tropical fish, she said, I chose an Agatha Christie novel. You both laughed, and you said to her, well done anyway, she was smiling, she said, well done yourself, you're awfully good at French, aren't you? You looked away to the side, shy and caught, you wanted to laugh or something, you said, yes, I am, I think.

Remember that, then, as you stop now, laughing into your hands in the rain, leaning against the wall of a grey office building in this beautiful city. Look around you in wonder again at where you are, remember the first night years ago when you went out with your prize book under your arm and her music still burning in your body, and all the walk home you saw the trees and how their branches met their leaves, the grass edging the pavement beneath your feet, the shabby lamp-posts reaching from the ground into the early night sky; you stopped and sat down where you were on the kerb between two parked cars, you knew the wheels, the smell of the oil, the drain full of litter next to you, the pitted surface of the road and the sky spread above you with its drifting cloud, and the words for every single thing you could sense around you in the world flashed through your head in another tongue, their undersides glinting like quicksilver. 🍎

James Meek

SURVIVAL AND THE KNEE

He woke up before dawn. That was OK. There was time to fall asleep, wake up, fall asleep, wake up again. He was on his own in a bed big enough for a couple of people, big enough to lie stretched out in all directions, trying to find cool parts of the sheet. Legs bent and arms bent, all the same way. He was lying there like a swastika, as well there was no-one to see. She was next door, in the next room, on her own in another bed. Asleep in the figure of a treble clef, head turned to one side, hair running black down the pillow. She'd promised to come with tea, but would she? A good thing would've been to take her the tea in bed and put it down by the bed and leave her alone with it, unless she asked different at the time.

He woke up again. What was it what was it what was it—a dream of standing on carpeted stairs, halfway down, looking at something like a framed picture on the wall, turned out to be an animated cartoon version of *New Society* magazine, consisted of red and yellow stickmen marching to and fro with brooms, sweeping.

She'd woken him, she'd come into the room and sat down on the edge of the bed, just sitting there looking at him. She was waiting for him to open his eyes and she'd smile. He opened his eyes. She wasn't there. The bedroom door was still closed. There was a square of sunlight glowing on the quilt. He moved his hand into it and felt the heat, he listened for the sound of her moving about.

He heard her coming down the hall. She knocked on the door. He closed his eyes. She knocked again. He became conscious of his heart. He became aware his lips were pressed together. She knocked again and opened the door. He felt the weight of her bare feet on the floorboards. She put a mug down on the floor beside the bed. He lay still with his eyes closed. She was standing there, still. His eyes were difficult to keep shut and he wanted to move. Even under the quilt he had to be looking tensed up. He started counting to ten in his head.

When he got to five she started to walk back to the door.

Thanks, he said, without moving or opening his eyes. She stopped.

I thought you were asleep, she said.

How could I drink the tea if I was asleep, he said. You were just going to let it sit there and evaporate. He opened his eyes. She was standing looking at him from the foot of the bed. She had a dressing gown on.

Time to get up, she said, it's really late.

Sit and talk to me while I drink my tea.

You spend too much time in bed.

She came and sat down on the edge of the bed. The fabric of the dressing gown made a quiet sound. She crossed her legs and her bare knee appeared out of the folds in a patch of sunlight.

God, your knee, he said, it's beautiful. He said it just as it came into his head. He wondered if she'd cover her knee up.

She frowned and looked down at her knee. She gathered the hair falling across her face with a single finger and flicked it behind. She looked at him. He glanced at her face and turned his eyes back to her knee.

It is, he said, it just is. Let me look a while.

Neither of them said anything for a time.

Enough? she said.

No, he said.

Your tea. Evaporation, she said.

I could look at your knee all morning.

It's five to twelve.

Shit.

Last night you said to bring you a cup of tea in the morning, not to show you my knee in the morning.

Why can't you smile, he said. You should be happy to have such a knee.

For God's sake, she said, you can't tell if I'm smiling or not if you're looking at my bloody knee.

He looked at her face. He smiled. She laughed and covered her knee.

Hey, he said, I was watching that.

Their eyes locked together. The laughter went slowly from her face. He felt his skin burning and had an erection, hidden under the folds of the quilt. She looked away.

Why did you want to look at my knee? she said.

It looked so beautiful.

Why?

It just did. Like a mountain or something. I don't mean like a mountain, I mean like a view from a mountain, a sunset or something, something you see that you think's beautiful and you want to look at it for a long time, even if there's no reason for it, it's not essential for survival or anything.

Oh yeah, she said. OK, I'll just chop my knee off and leave it on a plate on the bed, and that'd be lovely for you.

I think it'd go off, he said.

It's only because my knee's attached to my legs and my bum and the rest of me and you're thinking mannish thoughts about what leads on from the knee, she said.

He raised himself on his elbows. He reached down for the tea, lifted the mug to his mouth and drank. A hot dribble ran down his chest.

Fuck, he said.

Well? she said.

Well, if I was just wanting to look, not touch, just for the nice-lookingness of it, and you knew I was doing that, I wasn't peeping or staring at you in the street.

But you did want to touch.

Och, yes, I suppose, but . . . have you got a tissue or anything?

She folded her arms and looked at him without saying anything.

What? he said. He sighed and looked down. Heh. Tea chest! Look, I said what I thought, I meant it, your knee looked beautiful. It just came into my head, I said it, I meant it. I wanted, I mean, I don't know, is there not allowed to be lust anywhere?

Yeah, she said, getting up. Now it's lust. What happened to the mountains and the sunset.

I know what you're saying, he said. You're right but you're also completely wrong.

Yeah, she said, making for the door. It doesn't matter. Come on, get up, it's late.

It does matter.

The door closed.

It does matter. ❦

Naomi Mitchison

ON AN ISLAND

B y morning it was worse Kenny was. She herself had dozed off, for maybe an hour, between black night and the time when the lamp by the window began to look queer. The fire was down, but when she blew on it the peats flared again. The kettle would be boiling in a wee while. He would like a cup tea surely. Nothing to eat, the doctor had said. But how then would he keep his strength up? Maybe an egg—. From where she was by the fire she kept on looking back over her shoulder at him on the bed, not himself at all, a stranger in their own bed, in Kenny's body, pulling at the red blankets.

She made the tea, strong, with plenty of sugar, the way Kenny liked it. But the stranger pushed it away. She hardly knew whether to speak to him in the English or the Gaelic. But he answered to neither.

She looked out; it was low tide. The doctor would cross the ford easy. She had better see to the cow and the hens before he would be coming. Her mother came up past the back of the dyke. She looked at the stranger in the bed, and shook her head.

'Go you to the cow, Beitidh,' she said. 'I will sit with him. Will he not take his tea? Well, well. But it is a pity to waste a good cup.'

After she had fed the hens, Beitidh came back with the milk pail and set the half of it for cream.

'I will churn Saturday,' she said. 'He will be better then.'

For indeed it was a bonny fresh morning and she felt better herself, and that way she had a certainty that he too would be better. But her mother, sitting ben by the bed, gave her a look that spoilt that, and oh, now it came to her that Kenny would never dig his knife into the golden butter, never again, and she sat down on the wee stool by the window and put her head down in her hands, and she had cried the edge of her skirt wet through by the time she heard the doctor's car.

He did not speak much to her, only made her hold the lamp near, for it was kind of dark over by the bed. He was listening and feeling about, and Kenny began to moan, to make noises not like himself, not like Kenny, who was so strong and clever, and her hand shook, holding the lamp, and her mother's eyes on her were sorrowful and certain.

The doctor was speaking and at first she had trouble understanding him.

'But we havena been in an aeroplane, neither of the two of us,' she said. 'He would know—'

'He will not need to know,' said the doctor. 'And all you need to do yourself is to wrap him up warm. I will be with him to the hospital.'

'But—but then—how will I know?'

'You will just go over with Donny's van to Stronbost and you will get Mrs. Morrison at the Post Office to ring up the hospital,' he looked at his watch, 'round about four o'clock, and you will know then.'

'Och, I'm no' just sure—if I want him to go at all, Doctor—not so far—I will need to think it over!'

'Beitidh,' said the doctor, 'there is no time for thinking it over. The 'plane is on its way from Renfrew. Give me some safety pins now and we will wrap him up.'

She felt in the drawer for them blindly. He was taking Kenny away, she had no power to stop him. And what would they do with him at the hospital—och, she would never see him again!

The 'plane came down on the sand, and then, before she was used to it at all, the doctor and a strange kind of nurse had bundled Kenny in, with the red blankets round him, and he not saying good-bye, not knowing even they had taken him away. The door shut on her, and the thing left in a terrible wind and noise, and it was as though part of herself had been pulled away with it.

Her mother had everything straightened up within, and the bed made again, with her other blankets, the old plain ones that she used to sleep under before ever she was married on Kenny.

'If it is the Lord's will,' said her mother, 'we must not be the ones to complain. And maybe it is as well now that you have no bairns. For you will marry again, surely.'

Soon her sister came in and two more of the neighbours, and they put on the kettle again. 'Och, well, well, poor Kenny,' they were saying. 'He was a good lad. It was a terrible pity for him to be going this way.'

And she sat, half listening while they spoke of one or another who had died, either at home or after being taken away to the hospital. And the thing beat on her and now all the months of her life with Kenny had gone small and far. And she began looking

ahead, past the things that were to be done. For they would bring
back the corpse from the hospital as it had been done before with
others. It would come by the boat, and they would go down to meet
it. She would need to go to the store for a black dress; she had the
coat. There was money saved enough for everything. And of a
sudden she saw Kenny's hand putting the silver money into the jug
at the back of the press, Kenny's own strong hand, and she burst out
weeping and ran from the house. The rest looked on her with
compassion and fell again to speaking of the ways of death.

Donny's van was on the far side of the flood, and the boat would
be crossing, for it was high tide now. She took her place in the bows;
she must carry out the things the doctor had told her; she must
receive the news. Old Hamish had a web of tweed to ferry across,
but he put it and himself in the stern of the boat and was joined by
two of the crofters. They spoke in low voices, aware of her alone in
the bows.

She climbed into the van and the road went by and the dark banks
of peat and the dark shining water over the peat, and they came into
the long scatter of houses that was Stronbost, a few black houses
still, like their own, but mostly the new concrete ones. There had
been a time when she and Kenny had spoken together of how they
would build themselves a white house with a good chimney and
maybe a bathroom later on, and he would get the grant from the
Board. And that seemed all terrible long ago now.

She went into the store, and whispered to Mrs. Morrison how she
needed to telephone to the hospital, and could it be done. Mrs.
Morrison said it was the easiest thing in the world and brought her
to the telephone and spoke into the thing, and there was clicking
and slamming and then it was the hospital, and oh, it was beyond
her altogether to speak into it herself, to ask the question and to get
the answer! But Mrs. Morrison was brisk, she spoke, she asked. 'Here
is the doctor now,' she said. 'Speak you, Beitidh.' And then, calling
into the black mouth of the telephone, 'This is Beitidh here, Doctor.'

'He has been through the operation,' the doctor said, 'and he is getting on fine.'

'Oh, Doctor, Doctor!' said Beitidh into the thing, 'is it living he is? Is it living, my Kenny?'

'Aye,' said the doctor. 'Just that. We were in time.'

'Och,' said Beitidh. 'I thought—I thought—'

And then she began to laugh like a daft thing, and the black mouth of the telephone grinned at her, the way it could have been laughing too. ❦

Peter D. Robinson

THE WABE

The wind snapped at his ankles as the dark carnivorous mouth of the pub closed smoked-glass lips behind him. Turning up his collar against the November night, David climbed the hill under the wholesome light of the moon which retreated every forty yards behind the jaundiced reach of the streetlamps. As he lowered himself into their car—his car—he made a conscious effort not to open the passenger door. Five years of habit is not easy to break; painful to have broken.

Driving up the motorway, David thought about the pub. Its dimly lit corners where couples sat cocooned in false privacy under the eyes of sad, voyeuristic old men. He thought of the pillars from where the hunters selected and then stalked their prey. Where music pulsed deathlessly into the smoke-filled air, mingling with the scent of Leather and Paco Rabane. A bitter smile creased his face as he mentally re-ran the evening. On one hand, there were the faces he didn't know, some of whom were showing interest, indeed one had made an indifferent attempt at conversation, but he really couldn't drag up much enthusiasm for simultaneously pouring out their respective life histories, desperately seeking a common interest which could legitimise the 'coffee or something' question. On the other hand were the people he knew, the 'friends' who turned their faces away. They didn't want to talk. It was still too soon. It is always too soon to die! Far too bloody soon when your lover dies with you holding his hand to your face so that he, blind eighty-year-old incarcerated in a young man's body, can feel the tears you cry for him, for yourself, and for the doctors who told you in their ignorance that you had another year together.

That last time in hospital had been the best and the worst of it. Best because of Janet. Janet. A young, beautiful, strong nurse, humanely efficient, but with the herculean ability to shield from him the anxiety in her dusky eyes. Janet, whose jokes about night-sweats and bed-baths shouldn't have been funny, but were hilarious to them, vainly seeking a funny side to those most painful days: worst because the date and conditions for his return home changed almost daily and gradually receded into the fantasy world of the vaccine and the miracle drug. Towards the end even Janet ran out of one-liners as he ran out of time.

Even now David's mind ran with the hieroglyphic vocabulary of the disease: lymphocytes, pathogens, antigens, humoral and cellular immune responses, the non-functioning inner medullary space in the cortex of the lymph nodes, the opsonisation (or lack of it) by the dendritic macrophages of the pulp cords, twas brillig and the slithy toves did gire and gimble in the wabe. If ever he needed to give a lecture to the Boy Scouts on histology he wouldn't have to consult Gray's *Anatomy*. Ironic that one who felt nauseous to the point of collapse at the mention, never mind the sight of blood, and who had once fainted over the phone while making a dental appointment, should have spent two years drinking in everything he could read about bacteria, viruses, fungi, and multicellular parasites.

When he had been in Brussels and his 'other' had gone out on his blind date with destiny, David nightly sent a kiss through the air and did his best to hug the empty space beside him. Strange that for all the power of imagination, you can never re-create the touch, the physical contact between yourself and another. You would think that the nerve ends would remember what it is like to touch, but they don't. So while he lay touching himself in an effort to jog their memory, his other had welcomed into his body its tiny executioner. Not that there were any recriminations (spilt milk and all that). Anyway, each TV broadcast lengthened the dormant stage after exposure to the virus, so who could say for sure when it happened. They needed a scapegoat, however. A date. An act. The Brussels trip was as good as any. He had asked David to forgive him. Can you forgive someone for committing the sin which will tear you apart? It is either too foolish to consider, or beyond the limits of magnanimity. David realised that the car had stopped moving. Patting the steering-wheel, he thanked George, the auto-pilot of his subconscious, for getting him back safely and went reluctantly into the home which cried out for togetherness but found only half of together, which is alone.

A week later and he was back in the pub where each sought their Adonis and found only Narcissus. Just the experience of being in a place where everyone was like him; where the men loved men, and the women only women, gave him strength. He laved his soul in that elusive feeling of belonging even as he swore that this was a 'one drink and away' occasion. Later, he could never say when it was that the contact was made, he simply became aware that they were smiling at each other. The blond hair and almost white eyebrows, of which one was raised expectantly, were sufficiently contrary to his 'type' to warrant pursuit of the quarry, if only to conclude after the chase that he didn't want to follow the hunt to its logical conclusion.

They talked. Who remembers what is said in that first frenzied communication, as each tries to transmit their validity, their worth as a catch, to the other? They talked of summer (which was far away), of Paris (which was farther), of friends (who were being ignored), and they talked of sex, which was fast becoming an almost tangible current flowing between them. Eventually they spoke of everything and anything (even politics, which for David was unheard of), rather than be forced into the situation where they would have to fully say hello or really goodbye. David remarked on a modern paraphrase of the courtly style: 'The exquisite agony of sexual frustration which far outweighs the smoking of the post-coital cigarette.' They both laughed at that though neither of them smoked. Still laughing, they left the pub.

Half an hour's torrid conversation hardly qualified them to be called a couple, rather, two individuals, soldered without flux by need as much as desire.

Afterwards, when eventually the heartbeats had slowed, and the breathing relaxed, they talked again. This time it was less frantic. You don't need to impress someone whose sweat has mingled with your own. Intimacy of that kind, like noticing that he buys his underwear from Marks and Spencers too, removes all the barriers to conversation. So Andrew talked of his divorce, his kids, and his coming out, and David spoke of his coming out, his work, and, yes, of his dead lover. Somehow he felt it was all right, knew that he was at last being purged of the anger and at least the worst of the pain. 'Y'know,' he said, 'we slept together for five years. Safe sex? Didn't come into it. And I'm still fucking negative!' Things were a touch awkward then, for a bit, but a little more of what the pamphlets unimaginatively called body rubbing soothed the friction.

Over the months the need and desire for socialising apart diminished. One car took them everywhere while the other sulked in the garage. Even the two flats seemed not so much an extravagance, rather, one was becoming superfluous. They phoned the building society and asked for some bumpf on non-marital joint mortgages. Before return of post, Reality intervened. Andrew caught a cold, which developed into pneumonia and the bells started ringing in David's head. Sanity disintegrated in a rush of memories, and security slipped from their fingers via the phone call from the clinic which announced that an irregularity had been found in Andrew's blood. Irregularity! Why could they not be honest and say that the death warrant had been signed and sealed, and only awaited delivery? 'Something to do with helper-T cells,' Andrew said. David explained. He even managed a wry smile as he thought that at least his knowledge wasn't going to waste.

Test followed test, and slowly the mortar binding their lives together began to be washed away under the tide of waiting rooms and *Punch* magazines. They made running repairs as they went; a night at the theatre here, a new Billie Holliday album there, but it was a bit like putting a sticking plaster over an arterial fissure. The damage was done and no amount of cosmetic camouflage would dismiss it.

It was eventually discovered that Andrew's pneumonia had been only that: he was still positive, but the pneumonia had been the whole disease not just one symptom of a greater one. For all the shiny young doctor knew, Andrew could be one of the lucky ones who has the virus but never develops the disease. 'Or hasn't yet,' he added, shattering what little false hope they had allowed themselves.

Life went on. Not as normal; normal is not a word which sits easily with either Gays or AIDS, but it went on. David felt as though he had opened Life's binnacle only to find it empty. He intercepted the letter from the building society and slipped it under the mattress in the spare room. Andrew either guessed, or found it, or both, because he never once mentioned mortgages, who had been so keen at the outset. For weeks equilibrium returned—no one broke any mirrors anyway. Then David started having dreams, or rather had the same dream again and again.

He sat at the big kitchen table swinging his legs idly, stopping now and again to examine the scab on his knee. The worrying of this latest trophy caused him such a pleasurable pain, despite his mother's warning that if he played with it, it would never heal. His mother, a combination of woollens and silks, smells of baking and birthday scent, comforting softness and cutting scorn, came into the room and seeing David's idleness, immediately thought of something for him to do before the devil should. 'Will you go and get the eggs, Davey boy?' she asked in a tone which brooked neither refusal nor evasion. David rose with one last, successful tweak at his knee. The scab tore free and the comforting trickle of warmth wound its crimson way down his bare shin. He put on his duffel-coat, doing up the toggles with both hands. (He had never perfected the 'one-handed toggle-twist' as his elder brothers were quick to remind him.) He lifted the latch on the scullery door. 'Wellies!' boomed the voice of doom. (In his more philosophical moments David had come to the conclusion that adults had been placed on earth with the sole purpose of preventing children from getting dirty and thus enjoying themselves.) Once his wellies, and the required socks for padding, were on, David emerged from the industrious warmth of the kitchen into the sharpness of the morning.

The grey sky glared down on him as if it resented his intrusion. Half-closing his eyes against the light's indignation, he began to cross the yard. By some caprice of nature, large stretches of the ground were bone-dry while a few paces away lay inviting, gloriously adhesive pools of mud. Daffodils fought for nutrients as the hens battled for grain. Scattering before his approach, these chickens re-grouped, fluffing and re-arranging their dignity, crying out at the impudence of this two-leg.

A motley collection of old doors, warped planks and metal sheeting, the hen-house stood dejectedly in the middle of the yard. David approached quietly; the secret was not to alarm the layers—a frightened hen wouldn't lay, and while to his mother fewer eggs meant less to sell to the village shop, to David it meant spam sandwiches to take to school, something to be avoided at all costs. He entered silently, or as silently as one can open a door with creaking, rusty hinges and step on scattered old, dry straw.

The warmth and cooing contentment of the shadows welcomed David, but he had to shut his eyes for a moment to let them become accustomed to the gloom. He lifted a big Red from her stall and she clucked boastfully as he gently took up the alabastrine product of her womb. The egg shattered at his touch. He discarded it and wiped his hands free of the glutinous substance. Gingerly, with breath held, he lifted another egg. He almost managed to put it safely in his duffel-coat pocket before it crumpled in his hand. And so it went on. No matter how gentle he was, no matter how carefully he raised the eggs from their straw cushions, they shattered messily in his fingers. David woke trying vainly to wipe the viscous fluid from his hands like some latter-day Lady Macbeth.

When did the dream become reality? Gradually the fabric of their relationship came apart at the seams. Instead of riding out difficult patches with as much tolerance and understanding as he could muster, David's patience evaporated, and he would wade in with all guns blazing. Instead of saying 'Okay honey, let's see what we can do about this', it was 'It seems, Andrew, as if you are the one with the problem here'. The washing was thrown into the machine with a curse rather than the smile it used to get as he thought of the wearer of half the pile. He caught himself a couple of times on the phone, bitching about Andrew. That they had agreed to keep their troubles private, didn't seem to matter anymore.

Making love became having sex. Having sex became a chore. David tried to re-weave the magic: candles, a special meal, good wine; but the result was sex, not love. Formerly unimportant things began to take on new titanic significance. David's habit of idly flicking through the teletext pages while they watched television, Andrew's tendency to replace empty biscuit wrappers in the tin, these and others like them became the death throes of their relationship, which had once been the foibles of their love. They had played their hands well with the few aces they had been dealt, but David was fast losing his taste for the game. Simply wearing the same brand of underwear is no basis for a relationship. Or was that just an excuse? Was he not really just trying to get out, before he had to go through all the pain again? It wasn't really Andrew. Andrew was confused and hurting just as much as he. David didn't want to have to meet another Janet, didn't want to be left again as that half of together which is alone. ❦

Patricia Hannah

TINTIN IN EDINBURGH

A tweed jacket sprawled on the large double bed; from there a trail of clothing led past the Edwardian wardrobe, the dressing-table, the bookcase and two small armchairs, to end in a pair of grey trousers, crumpled like a deflated elephant on the floor outside the closed door.

Winifred hung Brockie's dress-suit over the wardrobe door to one side of the full-length mirror; she and Dab-it-off had done what they could with the stains. She paused to admire her reflection; that of a small thin woman (she'd say trim and not bad for sixty-five), wearing a white cotton slip, stockings and black court shoes. She put her cold hands to her face, hot from the steam of the iron then, refreshed, struggled with the clothes in the wardrobe until she freed a cocktail dress. She held it against her body and watched herself in the mirror smoothing out the creases in the full skirt of kingfisher blue taffeta. The dress was sleeveless with a matching bolero which forty years ago she would have slipped off to reveal smooth slim arms. The sweet susurrus of taffeta made her smile, and she swayed her hips and hummed a few bars of 'Begin the Beguine' as she carried the dress over to the bed and carefully laid it out.

From downstairs came the sound of a clock striking seven. Winifred stopped humming and called to the closed door, 'Are you all right? You've been in there for ages.'

'Yes,' came the answer from what had been a useful cupboard before it was converted into a bathroom.

Winifred sniffed the air, tiptoed to the bathroom door and sniffed again. 'Brockie! Are you smoking that pipe in there?'

'No.'

'Are you sure?'

'Yes.'

Winifred was suspicious; thirty minutes of silence in the bathroom meant pipe smoking or . . . 'You're reading!'

'What?'

She banged on the door. 'You're reading in there!'

'No I'm not!'

'What are you doing then, if you're not reading?'

Brockie sighed loudly. 'I'm minding my business and doing my business.'

'Are you constipated?'

'I'm contemplating!'

'For thirty minutes? You *are* constipated! I warned you about those Scotch eggs.'

'I didn't touch those Scotch eggs.'

'Then you must be reading. Tintin as usual? I'm going to check.'

She checked. She went to the bookcase, put on her glasses, sat on the floor and counted the Tintin books on the bottom shelf.

Behind her back, the bathroom door opened and a hand slipped a Tintin book under the discarded trousers. The door closed again, soundlessly.

Winifred pulled out 'Tintin in Tibet' to check the number of titles listed on the back and clucked with annoyance: the book was sticky with marmalade—lime marmalade. That would be Brockie, he loved the stuff. She smiled, remembering the visiting Swedish psychologist who'd misheard Brockie's answer, 'It's lime marmalade', and thought he was being offered slime for breakfast. That's what it would be tonight—slime in bits of puff pastry. Of course, they'd call them vol-au-vents, things sounded better in French, but the result would be indigestion; you could count on that.

She counted, and rose, triumphant. 'Twenty! There should be twenty-one!' Brockie didn't reply, a clear admission of guilt. With right on her side Winifred strode to the door. 'Brockie! You're a selfish old devil! You know I'm waiting to get in!'

The flush sucked and roared then faded to a gurgle. Winifred looked expectantly at the door—it stayed shut. Disappointment sharpened her anger; not only was she condemned to an evening of Californian wine and university catering instead of scrambled eggs in front of 'Casualty', but now she'd have to dress in a hurry, and live with the uneasy feeling that she'd forgotten to put on something essential. Bugger! 'Brockie! Let me in!'

'I'm shaving.'

'What?'

'Shaving!'

'For God's sake! I thought you'd done that!' Winifred retreated to the dressing-table, where she brushed her hair which flew and crackled under the bristles as if in sympathy with her thoughts. Why do I bother?—it's pipes and papers and penis envy everywhere.

Forty years of it, and no ecstasy. She threw down the brush. Three children, and no ecstasy. Vol-au-vents, and no ecstasy.

The bathroom door opened and Professor Brockie emerged. As Winifred had waned over the years, he had waxed into a stout old gent with red cheeks and black bush eyebrows. Wearing only a pair of voluminous boxer shorts and fluorescent green flip-flops, he sauntered across the room, a huge, bath-towel turban adding to his air of golden primeness.

He stopped, as if to acknowledge the acclaim of an invisible crowd, and declaimed: 'How was he changed from that Hector, who wended homeward, clad in the spoils of the Department of Psychology.'

'Right!' said Winifred. 'Where is it?'

'What?' asked Brockie, all innocence.

'The Tintin book!' She frisked him, but found nothing and pushed him out of the way. 'You knew I wanted my little plate,' she snapped as she slammed the bathroom door behind her.

Brockie sat down on Winifred's dress and removed his turban. Haroun Alrashid disappeared to be replaced by a tousled owl chick—fluffy white down sticking up in astonishment.

Winifred came out settling her dental plate in her mouth. 'I can't smile at the Principal without my little plate.' She grimaced horribly and clicked her teeth together. 'That's better. Now where did you hide it? Or have you flushed it down the pan?'

Brockie patted a damp spot on his leg with Winifred's dress. 'I told you I wasn't reading, what's all the fuss about?'

Winifred rescued her dress and hung it at the foot of the bed. Sitting down at the dressing-table, she smacked her face with a powder puff and her voice emerged from a honey-beige cloud. 'We're going to be late—they said eight o'clock.'

'You're fussing, Winnie. They can't start without me, I'm the guest of honour. You can't have a presentation if the presentee's not present.'

'What about Marlon Brando?'

'Has he been invited?'

'He refused to collect his Oscar, sent a Red Indian princess instead.'

'Well then, not much chance of him coming tonight. I don't know why they invite these fellows when they never bother to turn up.'

Winifred pencilled in a pair of eyebrows. 'I bet Marlon Brando doesn't read in the bathroom.'

'I bet he does, that's why he was late for 'Tosca' .'

'OSCAR! And he wasn't late, he didn't turn up.'

'I didn't know there was an opera called 'Oscar', but as we're not going to it there's no need to rush.' Brockie combed his hair. 'Really, Winifred, my working day is spent with disturbed people, I like a bit of peace and quiet in my own bathroom.'

Winifred applied bright red lipstick to her mouth. 'I spend the day with a disturbed house, and disturbed psychologists on the phone, and disturbed men at the door who want to sell me soap made by the blind with their feet.' She blotted her mouth on a tissue and stood. 'But do I get to spend the evening reading in the bathroom? Not bloody likely!'

'I hope you don't buy any of that stuff, Winnie.' Brockie sniffed his hands, 'Feet you say?' and stuck his head in the wardrobe. Winifred stomped from the room.

'I don't ask what you and Marlon Brando do when I'm not here . . .' Brockie wrestled with a tangle of coathangers. 'I do ask that I can come home after a tiring day and read Tintin in the lav without being made to feel like a criminal.' He emerged holding a white shirt. 'Where are my cufflinks, Winnie? Winifred!'

The vacuum cleaner, with Winifred on the end, rolled into the room. 'So you were reading Tintin.'

Brockie emptied a box of safety-pins and buttons onto the dressing-table and found his cufflinks. 'I didn't say that.'

She plugged in the vacuum. 'Yes you did. Just now, when I wasn't here.'

'Winifred, dear,' he inserted the cufflinks the wrong way round, 'how do you know what I said when you weren't here?'

She manoeuvered the vacuum into position. 'I heard you.'

Brockie turned the cufflinks, 'I was merely proffering an example; positing what I might want to do, not what I was doing.'

Winifred switched on the vacuum, 'I heard you.'

Brockie shouted above the roar of the motor, 'I can't hear you!' She ignored him, and he strode over to the wall and pulled out the plug. 'That's enough, Winnie! We don't have time for temperament, I have to be there for eight. It's my retirement party, everyone's coming—the whole Faculty of Medicine waiting with a set of Edinburgh Crystal decanters—and you decide to vacuum the carpet! I've come to expect a certain irrationality in your behaviour, but this is going too far!'

Winifred picked up the plug. 'We weren't in a hurry when you wanted to read Tintin. "They can't start without me"—remember?'

'Without me, Winnie.'

She banged the plug back into the socket and aimed the roaring vacuum at Brockie. He leapt sideways into the bathroom, and the vacuum sucked and choked on the trousers lying at the door. Winifred dragged them free, uncovering the Tintin book.

Brockie swaggered over to the bed, switching off the vacuum as he passed. 'Tintin locuta est; causa finita est!'

Winifred picked up the book. 'What?'

'Tintin has spoken; the case is concluded. You were the Latin scholar . . . The only female in the year who didn't look like Goebbels. We used to cut quite a dash at dances, me in my kilt and you all dolled up.' He promenaded with an imaginary partner, spun her round and knocked Winifred's dress to the floor. He kicked at it to free his feet. 'I hope you're wearing something nice tonight. It simply requires a wee bit of effort on your part. Where's that cocktail thing you used to wear? I liked that.'

'You're standing on it,' said Winifred.

Brockie looked down at the dress and stepped over it. 'No, no, not that. You could wear things like that once, but nowadays . . .' He fetched his suit. 'Do I have any black socks?'

Still holding the book, Winifred gathered up the dress and laid it to rest on a chair. She looked smaller and older; the Beguine had been and gone. The black socks were lying among the scattered pins on the dressing-table; she threw them at Brockie. They missed, and he hummed quietly and gleefully as he thrust one leg then the other into his trousers.

Behind his back, Winifred cracked Tintin's spine and pulled out the pages. She used the safety-pins to attach them, one by one, onto her slip.

Brockie put on his socks. He opened his mouth to ask for his shoes, but thought better of it and fished them out from where he'd left them, under the bed.

Around Winifred, Tintin searched for Red Rackham's treasure, but ran out of space long before he found it.

Brockie put on his jacket, felt in the pockets and pulled out a spotted bow tie and a long lost pipe. He clamped the pipe between his teeth, enjoying the reunion, then returned it to its pocket and tied his bow tie.

Winifred pinned two pages together to form a tube, and settled it firmly on her head. She looked at herself in the mirror. The hat wasn't quite right . . . She folded over the top and fastened it to the side. That was better—more French Revolution than Auto-da-fé. And the shoulders worked well—pinning the pages to her bra straps so they stuck out like epaulettes, gave her . . . Presence. Nice there was so much sea in the drawings—she was a Turquoise Presence, just like the Queen Mother. Winifred gave a radiant smile, picked up a black evening-bag and popped her compact, lipstick and comb inside. She snapped it shut, hung it in the crook of her elbow, and walked to the door. 'I'm ready, dear. Will I do?'

Brockie admired himself in the mirror. 'Fine, fine, now we really must get a move on—all your fussing has made us late.' He gently patted his groin to check all was in order. Not bad, he thought, not bad, and achieved without fuss. He made a point of never making a fuss. Career, marriage, children—no fuss. And after tonight—no fuss. There would be a bit of a fuss tonight, and then—no fuss. They'd hang Emeritus on him like a Do Not Disturb sign . . . No, he wouldn't fuss, it wasn't the end, it was a new beginning—the lion is dead, long live the old dog!

Brockie barked cheerfully at Winifred and Tintin, 'You found the dress, good. That colour suits you, I knew I was right.' He took her arm and led her towards the door. 'You think I don't notice after all these years; but I do.' ❦

Iain Crichton Smith

CHRISTMAS DAY

O n that Christmas Day, she was the only customer in the hotel for lunch. 'I shall take the turkey soup,' she said. The dining-room was very large and she sat at her table as if she was on a desert island. Above her head were green streamers and green hats and in the middle of the dining-room there was a green tree.

Somewhere in Asia the peasants were digging.

'The fact is,' she thought, 'I'll never see him again. He is irretrievably dead.' The pain was inside her like a jagged star.

There was this particular peasant with a bald head and when he was finished digging he went home to his family and played the guitar. It might have been China or Korea but when his mouth moved she didn't understand what he was saying. To think, she mused, that there were all these peasants in the world, and all these languages.

She drank her turkey soup and watched the two waitresses talking, their arms folded.

She had watched him die for three weeks. His pain was intolerable. After that there were the papers to be checked. One day she had left the house with a case and gone to the hotel in which she now was.

There were millions of peasants in the world and millions of paddy fields, and they all sang strange unintelligible songs. Some of them rode on bicycles through Hong Kong.

'I love you,' he had said at the end. Their hands had tightened on eternity. When she withdrew her hand the pulse was beating but his had stopped.

She wished to change her chair so that she could not see the waitresses, but she was naked and throbbing to their gaze.

When she had entered her room in the hotel for the first time she had switched on the television-set. It showed peasants working in the fields in the East. She had picked up the phone and wondered whom she could talk to. Perhaps to one of the peasants in their wide-brimmed hats. She had put the phone down.

There were twenty of them in the one house, children, parents, grandparents, aunts and uncles and they were all smiling as if their paddy fields generated light.

'I am thin as a pencil,' she thought. 'Why did I wear this grey costume and this necklace?'

She finished the turkey soup. Then she tried to eat the turkey. For me it was killed, with its red comb, its splendid feathers, its small unperplexed head on the long and reptilian neck. Nevertheless I must eat.

Wherever Tom had gone, he had gone. 'Put me in a glass box,' he used to say. 'I want people to make sure that I am dead.' But in fact he had been cremated. She heard that the coffins swelled out with the heat, but he had laughed when she had told him. 'Put me in an ashtray in the living-room.'

The smoke rose above the paddy fields and the peasants were crouched around it.

She left much of the turkey and then took ice cream which was cold in her mouth. She was alone in the vast dining-room.

Christmas was the loneliest time of all. No one who had not experienced it could believe how lonely Christmas could be, how conspicuous the unaccompanied were.

From the paddy field the peasant raised his face smiling and it was Tom's face.

'Hi,' he said in a fluting Korean voice.

The green paper hats above her swayed slightly in the draught which rippled the carpet below. It seemed quite natural that he should be sitting in front of her in his wide-brimmed hat.

'The heat wasn't at all unbearable,' he said.

He took out a cracker and pulled it. He read out what was written on the little piece of paper. It said, 'Destiny waits for us like a bus.' Or a rickshaw.

The world was big and it pulsed with life. Dinosaurs walked about like green ladders and bowed gently to the ants who were carrying their burdens. The peasant sat in a ditch and played his guitar and winked at her.

'I remember,' said Tom scratching his neck, 'someone once saying that the world appears yellow to a canary. Even sorrow, even grief.'

And red to a turkey.

She got up and went to her room walking very straight and stiff so that the waitresses' glances would bounce off her back. Who wanted pity when death was so common?

She sat on her bed and picked up the phone.

She dialled her own number and heard the phone ringing in an empty house.

'If only he would answer it,' she said. 'If only he would answer it.'
Then she heard the voice. It said, 'Who is that speaking, please?'
She knew it was Tom and that he was wearing a wide-brimmed
hat.

'I shall be home soon,' she said.

She took off her clothes and went to bed. When she woke up she
felt absolutely refreshed and her head was perfectly clear.

She packed up her case, paid her bill at the desk and went home.

When she went in she heard the guitar being played upstairs. She
knew that they would all be there, all the happy peasants, and sitting
among them, quite at home, Tom in his green paper hat with the
wine bottle in his hand. ❦

Dilys Rose

ALL THE LITTLE LOVED ONES

I love my kids. My husband too, though sometimes he asks me whether I do; asks the question, Do you still love me? He asks it while I am in the middle of rinsing spinach or loading washing into the machine, or chasing a trail of toys across the kitchen floor. When he asks the question at a time like this it's like he's speaking an ancient, forgotten language. I can remember a few isolated words but can't connect them, can't get the gist, don't know how to answer. Of course I could say, Yes I love you, still love you, of course I still love you. If I didn't still love you I wouldn't be here, would I, wouldn't have hung around just to go through the motions of companionship and sex. Being alone never bothered me. It was something I chose. Before I chose you. But of course that is not accurate. Once you become a parent there is no longer a simple equation.

We have three children. All our own. Blood of our blood, flesh of our flesh etc., delivered into our hands in the usual way, a slithering mess of blood and slime and wonder, another tiny miracle.

In reply to the question my husband doesn't want to hear any of my irritating justifications for sticking around, my caustic logic. He doesn't really want to hear anything at all. The response he wants is a visual and tactile one. He wants me to drop the spinach, the laundry, the toys, sweep my hair out of my eyes, turn round, away from what I'm doing and look at him, look lovingly into his dark, demanding eyes, walk across the kitchen floor—which needs to be swept again—stand over him as he sits at the table fingering a daffodil, still bright in its fluted centre but crisp and brown at the edges, as if it's been singed. My husband wants me to cuddle up close.

Sometimes I can do it, the right thing, what's needed. Other times, when I hear those words it's like I've been turned to marble or ice, to something cold and hard and unyielding. I can't even turn my head away from the sink, far less walk those few steps across the floor. I can't even think about it. And when he asks, What are you thinking? Again I'm stuck. Does it count as thinking to be considering whether there is time to bring down the laundry from the pulley to make room for the next load before I shake off the rinsing water, pat the leaves dry, chop off the stalks and spin the green stuff around the Magimix? That's usually what my mind is doing, that is its activity and if it can be called thinking, then that's what I'm doing. Thinking about something not worth relating.

—What are you thinking?

—Nothing. I'm not thinking about anything.

Which isn't the same thing. Thinking about nothing means mental activity, a focusing of the mind on the fact or idea of nothing and that's not what I'm doing. I've no interest in that kind of activity, no time for it, no time to ponder the true meaning of life, the essential nature of the universe and so on. Such speculation is beyond me. Usually when I'm asked what I'm thinking my mind is simply vacant and so my reply is made with a clear, vacant conscience.

I'm approaching a precipice. Each day I'm drawn nearer to the edge. I look only at the view. I avoid looking at the drop but I know what's there. At least, I can imagine it. I don't want to be asked either question, the conversation must be kept moving, hopping across the surface of our lives like a smooth flat stone.

Thought is not the point. I am feeling it, the flush, the rush of blood, the sensation of, yes, swooning. It comes in waves. Does it show? I'm sure it must show on my face the way pain might, the way pain would show on my husband's face . . .

—Do you still love me? What are you thinking?

Tonight I couldn't even manage my usual 'Nothing'. It wouldn't come out right. I try it out in my head, practise it, imagine the word as it would come out. It would sound unnatural, false, a strangled, evasive mumble or else a spat denial. Either way it wouldn't pass. It would lead to probing. A strained, suspicious little duet would begin in the midst of preparing the dinner and I know where this edgy, halting tune leads, I know the notes by heart.

(Practice makes perfect. Up and down the same old scales until you can do them without tripping up, twisting fingers or breaking resolutions, without swearing, yelling, failing or resentment at the necessity of repetition. Without scales the fingers are insufficiently developed to be capable of . . . Until you can do it in your sleep, until you *do* do it in your sleep, up and down as fast as dexterity permits. Without practice, life skills also atrophy.)

For years we've shared everything we had to share, which wasn't much at first and now is way too much. In the way of possessions at least. We started simply: one room, a bed we nailed together from pine planks and lasted a decade; a few lingering relics from previous couplings (and still I long to ditch that nasty little bronze figurine made by the woman before me. A troll face, with gouged-out eyes; scary at night, glowering from a corner of the bedroom). Money was scarce but new love has no need of money. Somewhere to go, to be together is all and we were lucky. We had that. Hell is love with no place to go.

While around us couples were splitting at the seams, we remained intact. In the midst of break-ups and break-outs, we tootled on, sympathetic listeners, providers of impromptu pasta, a pull-out bed for the night, the occasional alibi. We listened to the personal disasters of our friends but wondered, in private, in bed, alone together at the end of another too-late night, what all the fuss was about. Beyond our ken, all that heartbreak, all that angst. What did it have to do with us, our lives, our kids? We had no room for it. Nor, for that matter, a great deal of space for passion.

An example to us all, we've been told. You two are an example to us all. Of course it was meant to be taken with a pinch of salt, a knowing smile, but it was said frequently enough for the phrase to stick, as if our friends in their cracked, snapped, torn-to-shreds state, our friends who had just said goodbye to someone they loved, or someone they didn't love after all or anymore, as if all of them were suddenly united in a wilderness of unrequited love. While we, in our dusty, cluttered home had achieved something other than an accumulation of consecutive time together.

This is true, of course, and we can be relied upon to provide some display of the example that we are. My husband is likely to take advantage of the opportunity and engage in a bit of public necking. Me, I sling mud, with affection. Either way, between us we manage to steer the chat away from our domestic compatibility, top up our friends' drinks, turn up the volume on the stereo, stir up a bit of jollity until it's time to be left alone together again with our example. Our differences remain.

—Do you still love me? What are you thinking?

Saturday night. The children are asleep. Three little dark heads are thrown back on pillows printed with characters from Lewis Carroll, Disney and Masters of the Universe. Three little mouths blow snores into the intimate bedroom air. Upstairs, the neighbours' hammer tacks into a carpet, their dogs romp and bark, their antique plumbing gurgles down the wall but the children sleep on, their sweet breath rising and falling in unison.

We are able to eat in peace, take time to taste the food which my husband has gone to impressive lengths to prepare. The dinner turns out to be an unqualified success: the curry is smooth, spicy, aromatic, the rice dry, each grain distinct, each firm little ellipse brushing against the tongue. The dinner is a joy and a relief. My husband is touchy about his cooking and requires almost as much in the way of reassurance and compliments in this as he does about whether I still love him or not. A bad meal dampens the spirits, is distressing both to the cook and the cooked-for. A bad meal can be passed over, unmentioned but not ignored. The stomach, too, longs for more than simply to be filled. A bad meal can be worse than no meal at all.

But it was an excellent meal and I was wholehearted and voluble in my appreciation. Everything was going well. We drank more wine, turned off the overhead light, lit a candle, fetched the cassette recorder from the kids' room and put on some old favourites: smoochy, lyrical, emotive stuff, tunes we knew so well we didn't have to listen, just let them fill the gaps in our conversation. So far so good.

Saturdays have to be good. It's pretty much all we have. Of us, the two of us just. One night a week, tiptoeing through the hall so as not to disturb the kids, lingering in the kitchen because it's further away from their bedroom than the living-room, we can speak more freely, don't need to keep the talk turned down to a whisper. We drink wine and catch up. It is necessary to catch up, to keep track of each other.

Across the country, while all the little loved ones are asleep, wives and husbands, single parents and surrogates are sitting down together or alone, working out what has to be done. There are always things to be done, to make tomorrow pass smoothly, to make tomorrow work. I look through the glasses and bottles and the shivering candle flame at my husband. The sleeves of his favourite shirt—washed-out blue with pearly buttons, last year's Christmas present from me—are rolled up. His elbows rest on the table which he recently sanded and polished by hand. It took forever. We camped out in the living-room while coat after coat of asphyxiating varnish was applied. It looks good now, better than before. But was the effort worth the effect?

My husband's fine pale fingers are pushed deep into his hair. I look past him out of the kitchen window, up the dark sloping street at parked cars and sodium lights, lit windows and smoking chimneys, the blinking red eye of a plane crossing a small trough of blue-black sky. My house is where my life happens. In it there is love, work, a roof, a floor, solidity, houseplants, toys, pots and pans, achievements and failures, inspirations and mistakes, recipes and instruction booklets, guarantees and spare parts, plans, dreams, memories. And there was no need, nothing here pushing me. It is nobody's fault.

I go to play-parks a lot, for air, for less mess in the house, and of course because the kids like to get out. Pushing a swing, watching a little one arcing away and rushing back to your hands, it's natural to talk to another parent. It passes the time. You don't get so bored pushing, the child is lulled and amenable. There's no way of reckoning up fault or blame or responsibility, nothing is stable enough, specific enough to be held to account and that's not the point. The swing swung back, I tossed my hair out of my eyes and glanced up at a complete stranger, a father. The father smiled back.

We know each other's names, the names of children and spouses. That's about all. We ask few questions. No need for questions. We meet and push our children on swings and sometimes we stand just close enough for our shoulders to touch, just close enough to feel that fluttering hollowness, like hunger. We visit the park—even in the rain, to watch the wind shaking the trees and tossing cherry blossoms on to the grass, the joggers and dog-walkers lapping the flat green park—to be near each other.

Millions have stood on this very same ledge, in the privacy of their own homes, the unweeded gardens of their minds. Millions have stood on the edge, and tested their balance, their common sense, strength of will, they have reckoned up the cost, in mess and misery, have wondered whether below the netless drop a large tree with spread branches awaits to cushion their fall. So simple, so easy. All I have to do is rock on my heels, rock just a shade too far and we will all fall down. Two husbands, two wives and all the little loved ones. 🍎

Kay West

THE SINGLE BED YEARS

I remember the day you called, when I dashed to the 'phone clad in my greens and yelled my news to Tom who happened to be passing that you'd got it, you'd got it! Tom and I danced up the corridor in our white bloodstained clogs and clattered into theatre three only to be frowned upon by Sister Mack as we both sat jubilantly discussing my news. At lunch I'd sat oblivious to everything except my own thoughts, not knowing how I'd survive the month till I'd be with you. Oh and the blissful headache of organising a transfer, of packing and persuading my very sensible father to become a removal firm for an evening. I remember going back to my room in the nurses' home and quelling my immediate need for you and then bells rang and there was your soft northern voice at the end of the line.

So I arrived in the month of September with my father littering your living room with boxes, suitcases and rucksacks. You looked on horrified while I tried to persuade you between staff farewell party hiccups that I had indeed tossed out my junk. I stood clutching my handbag, avoiding your penetrating gaze as my father cast curious glances from behind a packing box.

Later, after my father and I had eaten your carefully prepared salad (he was disappointed, he wanted to sample the famous northeast fish supper) and he had retreated to the west coast in his immaculate BMW, we were finally alone and I took you my flatmate, my landlady into my arms. I breathed your exquisite perfume, kissed your aquiline nose and you laid your head on my breast and stared disdainfully at my scattered belongings.

It was late when we finally reached bed, only after you insisted that I unpack and your washing machine accumulated a dozen pairs of dirty denims. You worried that the neighbours would think that a man had moved in when they saw them on the washing-line the next day.

Oh but lady! Blue eyes! The bed! I could not conceal my disappointment when a single bed blinded my vision and you stood naked apart from your mini briefs and insisted it was the largest single bed in town. I asked if you had taken a tape measure as you bashfully explained the shopping trip with your ageing mother, who was after all paying for this piece of treasured furniture, the assistant's confusion as you had said a double, your mother a single and the assistant's wicked snigger as your mum demanded the reason for your need of a double bed. Blue eyes, I could envisage it all as your face became the colour of the plush maroon carpet. You said the single bed would be cosier for us and I agreed as we hurriedly satiated our passion and then you added that we'd have the rest of our lives as you saw me quizzically glance at the mere quarter hour that had passed on the clock. I had slept dreaming about the rest of our lives in a single bed.

A couple of months passed. We settled into a routine like newly weds. We argued over the housework. I cooked while you dusted every speck of dust you could find and deplored my nicotine habit which was to your way of thinking increasing your amount of chores. Yet we shared our baths, our passions and tins of lager and packets of peanuts and watched the soap operas. I introduced you to literature and chilli con carne while you went to work on my wardrobe and appointed yourself my personal accountant.

I met your family, introduced as your flatmate of course, and your straight friends whom I instantly disliked. We entertained gay couples with cheap liebfraumilch and chilli and discussed the gossip of the week. You'd trail guests round your new flat, briefly stopping in 'your' bedroom as the heterosexuals admired the decor and the homosexuals gazed amazedly at the single bed.

Winter arrived and with it my family for a tour of inspection under the guise of my birthday. We hurriedly made a makeshift bedroom out of the boxroom installing a z-bed and some of my junk, then you sat and worried. I puffed languidly on my cigarette, unearthed my moussaka recipe, vexed I would be unable to spend my birthday night with you.

I will never forget my mother's arrival as she swept past your astonished face and conducted her own tour. She peered out the kitchen window, stopped off in the loo before she entered 'your' bedroom at which she disinterestedly glanced round. She flung open the door to 'my' bedroom and stopped short while I had flung the door back with a comment of 'just my usual mess, mum!'

Do you remember how relieved we were when they left and we sank thankfully into our single bed? We stretched its springs as we stretched our bodies and you tried to smother my passions with the pillow for fear the deaf old lady next door would hear. I still laugh as I recall your stunned expression when I expounded another of my 'they must know' theories. I reminded you of the same single sheet, pillowcase and kingsize continental quilt cover which hung faithfully every fortnight on the communal green to dry in a billowy north-east wind.

A year or so passed. We continued to share our lives, our baths, our passions and the single bed. Holidays were spent in twin-bedded hotel rooms with the customary half hour employed energetically crumpling the sheets of the unused bed before a maid knocked on the door. Christmas arrived once again and we showered each other with gifts expensive and not so expensive. We cooked our own turkey, drank French red wine and retired to the single bed early. I remember sitting inebriated at your family Christmas dinner, tossing off liqueurs while you apprehensively watched my every move and evaluated my conversation. I watched your uninhibited delight as you unwrapped your presents and almost kicked myself as I nearly thanked your sister for giving you an electric blanket (single size of course!).

Months later we weren't on speaking terms as I impulsively indulged my maternal instincts and bought a dog and changed our comfortable lives overnight. I had tried to persuade you that it was easier than my having a baby. You had sat aghast and distressed as you sought for the plausible answer to your family's imminent question of how you, the landlady, could allow your headstrong flatmate to bring a dog into your home. Luckily they were charmed by her, just as you were and you came to love her despite the puddles that appeared on the carpet.

We were a family now and we shared our lives with our little friend, our home, our food, our packets of peanuts and the single bed. In the morning when she woke she'd bound through to the bedroom and with a leap like a high jumper she'd land across your shoulders, and you'd curse and grunt and tell me I should take her walkies even though it was only five a.m. Instead I'd try and squeeze her into the remaining available space.

Blue eyes, believe me when I say I cursed too as I'd try and pull your warm body closer while the dog wriggled between us and fought for her share of the pillow. Amorous a.m.'s were evicted from our lives and the bed linen was promoted to a weekly wash.

It all got too much in the end. We both woke with aching muscles and stiff spines as the single bed refused two adults sprawling space. We argued over the unthinkable—buying a double bed as we lay in our single but couldn't think of a suitable excuse. We thought a double bed too obvious and you argued that our personal comfort was a selfish consideration. Think of how hurt your family would be when truth met their eyes as they saw 'your' new bed. We somehow actually reached the stage of debating who would pay. You pointed out that you had bought the flat and the leather suite. I had to remind you of a recent shopping trip of mine when you sent me out for bread and milk and I had come back with a three-year-old Ford Fiesta acquired on hire purchase. But it was the vision of us both shyly bouncing our buttocks in front of a harassed Saturday salesman and the odd stares from milling shoppers that had us finally rejecting the idea, and so we faithfully continued to clamber into the single bed each evening.

Yet I needed time to think so I packed my bags and set off for suburban Glasgow and a week of family quibbles and a concerned father as I hit the city nightspots and staggered in at breakfast time. As was expected I didn't last the week. I upset the household routine and the daily help handed in her notice.

So I arrived home and changed your immaculate flat into chaos once more as I unsuccessfully attempted to unpack my haphazardly packed bags. You expertly and skilfully arranged the loads for the machine and I gave you a present of rock which I knew you would hate and I would eat later.

Yet I had the time to think during my brief holiday and told you that enough was enough and no longer could I tolerate the confines of the single bed and all that it represented of our lives. Something had to change and again we launched into long tedious discussions of double beds, your paranoia and my seeming boldness. The discussion became rage which lasted an hour, with the dog refereeing from under the settee until I slammed out of the flat, the dog whimpering at my heels.

Do you remember, Blue eyes, when I 'phoned you hours later and told you that I'd got it, I'd got it? You snapped back down the static, 'got what?' and slammed the 'phone down. I raced back to the flat and successfully persuaded a very disgruntled you to participate in my mystery tour.

I will never forget the look of amazement on your face as I conducted the tour round the quiet semi that had two double bedrooms, with ample space for two double beds, and a much needed back garden for the dog. Nervously, Blue eyes, I had looked at you, unable to penetrate your business-like stare as you surveyed the property and held up a questioning finger of dust from the window sill. Seconds later your blue eyes had sparkled and smiled and we shook hands on our deal and hurried back to the single bed.

By the end of that summer we had moved and settled into our semi and more importantly our double bed. Yet it wasn't long after that we found ourselves staring at each other across the extra space, gave chaste little kisses and went our sprawling separate ways and slept. And I slept dreaming of the single bed years. 🍏

James Robertson

WHAT LOVE IS

Something in the light changes, and Dan, who is not long home from his work, realises it has started to snow. He goes from the kitchen to the front room of the flat and stands at the bay window, looking down on the traffic and the orange glow of the streetlights. A small thrill shivers through him as he watches the first flakes pass by. It's like being a child again. A gust of wind blows the snow upwards, and the falling flakes mix with the rising. Dan looks into the cloud-laden sky over the grey city. He sees it as a great sagging mattress stuffed with tiny feathers. The mattress has burst and there are feathers everywhere. He looks at his watch. It's half-past five. He thinks about Joan coming back on the bus through the snow, but she won't leave her work until after seven. He has a couple of hours.

Amazing what you can see through windows. Once, through this very one, he saw a woman fly. She lived on the other side of the street, on the other side of the constant stream of cars and taxis and buses, in a fourth-floor flat. She cleaned her windows by climbing out on the ledge and holding on to the frame while she wiped and polished. Forty feet above the traffic she stood on a ledge six inches wide, and Dan could hardly bear to look at her. He closed his eyes because she frightened him, balancing there, and he saw the arc of her body falling backwards and being held like a sheet of paper in the air and then suddenly her gift of flight—this being the only way to save her—and when he opened his eyes again the window was closed and the woman gone.

Another time, he was washing his breakfast things in the kitchen sink before leaving for work, and across the back-greens he saw a young woman doing the same, directly opposite but one floor down. As his hands moved in the bowl of soapy water he saw her stop and lower her head. She was wearing a white blouse and he saw her fingers, which must, like his, have been wet, go to touch the front of it. Then she reached for a towel, wiped her hands, and swiftly unbuttoning the blouse she slipped it off. She must have spilt something on it, coffee or marmalade or something. She held a corner of the towel under the tap for a moment, and he watched her dab at the blouse with it. He imagined the tops of her breasts curving out of her bra—it was too far for him to really see this—her hair falling forward, her breasts rising and falling as she worked at the stain—even through two lots of glass she seemed very alive to him. After a minute she held the blouse up to the light, then draped it over one arm and left the room. Tears sprang into Dan's eyes. He was leaning hard up against the sink unit. He took his wet hand away from himself. Sex. That was what he wanted. He couldn't, though. He couldn't go back to bed. He couldn't wake Joan because she was on the late shift and would want another hour's sleep. He felt guilty because in any case he didn't want to have sex with Joan, he wanted it with a woman across the way, in another room in another flat in another life.

Dan isn't frightened of other lives. He imagines them all the time. The only life he is frightened of is his own.

Every morning, whether she is on the early shift or the late one, Joan takes a bus to her work. She works from eight till five or ten till seven, and she does a morning every third Saturday as well. She would drive to work if they owned a car, but they can't afford one. She learned to drive when she was eighteen, in her father's car, and she passed her test first time. She needs this skill for her job. She works on the reservations desk of a car-hire firm. Self-drive, to use the jargon. She has to be able to drive the cars from one area of the forecourt to another, and park them in confined spaces. The self-drive desk is only one part of the place, which is a big Ford dealer's. There is a showroom for new models and a parking-lot full of secondhand ones, and there is the self-drive desk. Joan has been there for fifteen years.

Other lives disturb Joan. The bus is full of them, different ones at different times of the day, and when she finds herself thinking about them she does her best to block them out. She doesn't want them to encroach. Her life may not be perfect but it is hers and she has it worked out, the routine of it. The routine is what keeps her going; she will not allow it to oppress her.

'How was your day?' Dan asks her. He is cutting up vegetables for tea. He cooks the tea on the days when she is on the late shift.

'Just the usual,' she says. Once—only once—Dan went to see her at her work. It was a summer afternoon and he decided to walk at least part of the way home. It wasn't much of a detour to go by the

Ford dealer's place. Afterwards he wished he hadn't. There were three women on the self-drive desk, Joan and two others. They were dealing with five customers and all the phones were ringing. The women were making bookings, taking money or credit cards, inspecting driving-licences, explaining the insurance, checking that returned cars had full tanks, taking customers to their cars and demonstrating the controls to them. Whenever they got out from behind the desk they seemed to be about to break into a run. Their manner was polite, efficient and subservient. All of the customers were men. Dan stood just inside the door watching this scene for a few minutes, without Joan seeing him. Thirty feet away, a couple of sharp-suited salesmen were standing about in the showroom. They were doing nothing, and seemed oblivious to the frantic activity of the women. Occasionally one of them would run his finger along the roof or bonnet of one of the new cars, as if to demonstrate his expertise, his familiarity with the merchandise. They paid Dan no attention because he did not look like someone with the money to buy a car. This was true. Several of the models on display cost more than his entire year's salary. He quietly left before Joan saw him. He never mentioned to her that he had been there.

'Just the usual,' she says, and Dan is horrified and ashamed that his wife has done that job for fifteen years. He chops the carrots with a vengeance.

Yvonne at his work keeps lecturing him, in a friendly, good-intentioned way. 'You're too willing,' she tells him. 'You're too conscientious. Nobody should have to put up with the amount of work they give you.'

Yvonne herself is no slacker. She's the receptionist. Apart from not having to deal with the cars, her job is as frantic as Joan's. She fields the phone-calls and the visitors and does some typing and she even finds time to give Dan advice. She is twenty-two—half his age—but she doesn't see any irony in giving advice to a man old enough to be her father. Dan's official job-title is Requisitions Manager. The firm—a small but industrious firm of architects—gave him this name and a ten per cent rise after he'd been with them for five years and Storeman had become too much of an understatement to be ignored. As well as running the stores, Dan is in charge of repairs, equipment, the post-room, and health and safety. He is responsible for the maintenance and cleaning contracts and the stationery purchases, and often he acts as a courier, delivering documents to other locations in the city. When he has a spare half-hour he'll sometimes work the switchboard to let Yvonne get on with something else. He is indispensable to the firm, and this gives him enough satisfaction to offset the nagging feeling that he is underpaid and overworked. Yvonne, who is not long out of college and is afraid of no one, fuels his suspicions. 'They take advantage of your good nature,' she says. 'They exploit you, you know they do. You shouldn't let them.'

Dan at home. He has a big record collection. He loves the sound of a woman singing, and it doesn't much matter to him if it's Jessye Norman or Mary Black or Nina Simone. There's something about any woman's voice which is worth listening to. That's what he thinks. But most of all he listens to Billie Holliday. He could listen to her sing for hours and think only minutes had gone by. He has about twenty different albums of Billie Holliday, many of them with different recordings of the same song, little variations that he has become totally familiar with—so that he can listen to a song and say, 'Yes, with Ray Ellis and his orchestra, 1958 sessions.' Joan likes Billie Holliday too, but she gets irritated by this perfectionism. 'Sometimes I think you don't listen to the songs themselves any more. You listen for the bits that are missing.' Dan gives her his smile, the one that says, yes, you're right, but you don't know anything. 'You don't know,' Billie sings, 'what love is, until you've learned the meaning of the blues.' What a life, thinks Dan, alone in the front room at two in the morning, what a life she had to have, to sing like that.

Joan sits on the bus and different lives come at her, veering away at the last moment. She tries to be untouched by them, but it's hard. One morning there are three Asian girls going into town. Their hair is thick and black—she can imagine how heavy it must feel just by looking at it—but their loose black silk trousers look lightweight. Although young they seem very dignified, aloof even. She is not a racist, but she is sure of one thing: their lives and hers have nothing in common.

Another time, coming home in the evening, it's three white girls. They are loud but at the same time conspiratorial, trying to impress the bus with their grown-up talk, which is about the different stages of undress they have reached with their boy-friends. Joan, who could be their mother, is embarrassed and intrigued. She can't stop herself listening. Then a woman of her own age stands to get off the bus, and as she passes the girls her rage comes pouring out: 'You're disgusting! Decent people having to listen to your filth! Dog-dirt! You're worse than dog-dirt!' 'Piss off!' the girls chorus as she steps off the bus. Joan finds herself turning to watch the woman disappear on the crowded pavement.

One day there's an old drunk man giving the world view to everybody on the bus. It's only mid-morning but already he's had a skinful. 'Too many people 'assatrouble. Westafrica'neastafrica'ntha. Six families tae a hoose. The Ashian shituashion. I know, I know.' The other passengers seem to find him funny. He's a Scotch comedian pretending to be a drunk. They nod and smile and shake their heads to one another. Joan is alone.

Then one night, with winter coming on, she gets on the bus to come home and as soon as she sits down at the back she knows she has done the wrong thing. There are three boys just in front of her—all these young lives seem to come in threes—and apart from them the lower deck is empty. They are busy carving up the seats. She should get up and move to the front but she doesn't want to draw attention to herself. She listens to the blades slicing through plastic. The bus stops and an Inspector gets on, a Sikh. 'Oh, here we go,' says one of the boys, 'a fucking towelheid. Eh, lads, feet up on the fucking seats.' Joan sits mesmerised. The Inspector is a middle-aged man with a full, greying beard. He comes down and checks their tickets, then hers. As he goes back past them he says, 'Take your feet off the seats, please.' He can't help but see the ripped covering. 'Fuck off ya black cunt ye.' He calmly walks to the front of the bus, where he speaks first to the driver, then into his radio. At the next stop the boys run off the bus.

Joan breathes out. The air is so oppressive. She just sat back, shrank back in her seat and hoped it wouldn't touch her. She has to admit her fear.

It's not just that she is frightened about things like that. She thinks about what she is becoming, has become. She keeps telling herself that she could be a lot worse off, that she and Dan have a roof over their heads and two jobs that are secure and a holiday every year (not that they go away, but the option is there) and all right it would be nice to have children but she doesn't really know if it would be, she just says that because it's expected of her, not that anyone ever says, 'Wouldn't you like children?', she wouldn't think much of someone who came out and asked as personal a question as that, not after all this time. But she can't avoid the truth. She can cope with her own life now simply because, at some point, she can't remember when, she lost the courage to change. It's not that she doesn't have fear—she has. It's that she doesn't have courage.

And what would her children be? Like those boys, those girls? It's too late, but she can't help wondering.

Yvonne says to Dan, 'You've got to put your foot down. Brian abuses you, Diane exploits you. You're exploited. I mean, we all are, but we get paid enough for it. You do far more than you need to for them. Coming in at the weekend last week. Staying on to change her office around for her. They don't even thank you for it. You're a really nice man, everybody likes you, we only want to see you getting fairly treated.'

'I'm all right,' he tells her. 'I appreciate your concern, but really I'm all right. I'm quite happy doing that kind of thing.'

Although they don't own a car Dan and Joan have a problem with car ownership. Many of the neighbours who have cars have had them fitted with alarms, and the alarms keep going off, usually at two in the morning. Dan hates them. 'It's just blatant selfishness,' he rants. 'Every time they go off they're saying, I'm looking after Number One, don't touch, I've commandeered the space in and around this tin box and if the wind buffets it or someone knocks it trying to squeeze by to get to the pavement and your sleep's disturbed that's tough, that's not my problem.' Joan says: 'They have to protect their property. I know what you mean, but they have to do something.' 'They're noise pollutants,' says Dan. 'Those alarms going off is a worse kind of pollution than the exhaust fumes.' One night Dan's going to sort them. He'll go down into the street in his pyjamas and take a hammer to the windscreen of the screaming car, and for good measure he'll smash in the headlights flashing in time with the alarm. 'Now you've something to make a fucking noise about,' he'll shout. And all the people leaning out of their windows in their nightwear, the non-carred, cheering and applauding.

Joan at work. One of the salesmen is called Maurice. The first thing to notice about Maurice is his hair. It stands upright and waves like a cornfield in the breeze. It does this by design not by nature. He keeps it corn-coloured too and it looks absurd on a fifty-year-old. Margaret, who works with Joan, christened him The Coxcomb, and they all take the piss out of him, but Maurice is immune to anything that might alter his own good opinion of himself. If you're on your knees in front of the filing cabinet Maurice is the guy that always says, 'Say one for me when you're down there, love.' Or if you're not wearing your best smile he'll say, 'Cheer up, it might never happen.' At quiet moments he deigns to lean on their counter, practising his chat-up lines. As soon as a customer appears he skates off again: 'A woman's work is never done, isn't that right, Joan?' 'It's well seen a man's work never gets started in here,' says Margaret. But Maurice can make a sale in twenty minutes and float back with his ego refuelled. An Asian man approaches the desk. 'Oh-oh,' says Maurice under his breath, 'looks like you'll be trading on the black market this afternoon, ladies.' 'What was that, Maurice? I didn't quite catch that,' Margaret calls after him, but Maurice is back among the new cars, on his own territory.

The women are talking about *Thelma and Louise* one day. It's not long out on video. Margaret's saying, 'It's brilliant, the way she lets that bastard have it,' and suddenly Maurice is there, sidling in.

'Is that the film about the two lezzies?'

'No, Maurice, it's not,' says Margaret.

'Only joking,' he says, 'I saw it myself. Liked the music.'

'Oh, just the music?'

'Well, some of the rest of it was a bit O.T.T. if you want my opinion.'

'Did you not think he was asking for it, then?'

'Oh, now, I'm not saying he was right, of course I'm not. The guy was out of order, no question.'

'He was raping her, for God's sake,' says Margaret.

'Ay, but he backed off. I mean, she shot him after he'd backed off. A bit strong, surely.'

'Sounds fair enough to me,' says Joan. She's amazed at herself. She hasn't even seen the film.

'Joan, I'm disappointed in you,' says Maurice. 'I didn't think you were into women's lib. All these years we've worked together, Joan, and I never knew you were for burning your bra.'

'You're pathetic,' says Joan, 'if that's what you think women's lib is about. You're pathetic anyway.' She can't believe she said that. Neither can Maurice. He retreats, pink-faced, the coxcomb bouncing ludicrously. Margaret hoots derisively at his back. 'Imagine being married to it,' she says.

And Joan feels good. She suddenly feels alive. She feels sorry about telling Dan to stop moping about with Billie Holliday. She wants to speak to him, to tell him that they do know what love is, they've just let it get buried somewhere along the way. As soon as she gets a quiet moment she's going to phone him, just to see if he's home, just to let him know she's thinking about him. All this distance they've let come between them, a lot of it's her fault, she wants to try and break it down. Maybe they could move away, start again somewhere where no one knows them. Maybe it's not yet too late.

Twice, sometimes three times a week, Dan has the flat to himself for a couple of hours. And one Saturday morning in three. These times are good for listening to records, reading the paper, watching something on the telly that Joan doesn't like or approve of. And sometimes they're good for other things.

Sometimes Dan gets out his magazines. The best bit about the magazines is after you buy them but before you start to read them. Even before you get home, walking back with them under your jacket, it's like you've bought an entry into another life. At this point they can contain anything, anything you want them to. The perfect woman might be in there, the woman that's perfect for you. It's only once you read them that the disappointment sets back in. You're always disappointed. The other life never lives up to your expectations. This is the nature of the magazines, their purpose, to leave you dissatisfied and send you back, sooner or later, for more. Dan understands this, but it doesn't stop him doing it.

Lately some of the magazines have started advertising phone-lines. Lately Dan has started reaching for the phone. It's a new thrill, he knows it won't last for ever. But just for now he likes what he hears, the security of the women's voices, the repetition of familiar phrases. He likes the posh voices that say, you can suck my nipples, and the taunting voices that say, get down on your knees and beg for it, but most of all he likes the close, breathy voice that says, I'm glad you're here and we're all alone. . . . It's pathetic really, he knows what a con it is. Maybe it's this, and not the loneliness in the woman's voice, that sometimes brings the tears after he has come.

All Dan wants is something else, for life to be something more than what it is. He is a nice man, a decent man. Really he is. But when he looks in the bathroom mirror, cleaning up, he does not much like what he sees.

Joan has a breathing-space, a lull. No phones ringing, nobody returning their car. Outside, the air thickens. She dials the number. In the space before the connection is made, she wonders if he'll answer, if he got home before the snow. She hopes so. She hopes he is safe. She wants everything to be all right. ❦

Susan Chaney

FIRST LOVE

argot Rose Tremain was my first love. For a long time
I loved her as passionately as I loved God, in fact I loved her more because
Margot Rose, unlike The Almighty was a strictly forbidden pleasure.

'You're not to play with that girl,' said my mother. 'She's common.
She lives on the council estate and she speaks so badly, I wouldn't
want you picking up that awful accent. Her mother's no better than
she should be.'

'I think her mother is very nice,' I replied. 'I think she looks lovely
with her suntan and her gold earrings. I think she looks sort of
foreign and mysterious like a gipsy.'

'It's ridiculous for a woman her age to dress the way she does. She has terrible varicose veins and she doesn't seem to care who sees them. She should spend less time sunning herself on the beach and more at home looking after her family. It's really quite disgraceful the way she lets those girls run wild with those awful names she gives them, they're bound to get into trouble. I shouldn't be surprised if they were all pregnant before they were sixteen.'

I thought the Tremain girls all had beautiful names, there was Margot Rose, Lucinda, Loveday and Camelia. They were all infinitely preferable to my own which was Hilary. Hilary! It sounded so dull and plodding like marmite and semolina pudding, brown bread and everything else that was good for me. It seemed to me to be the epitome of all that was hateful in my life, of all that was sensible and respectable and suffocating. It evoked Peter Pan collars, smocked dresses and Start-rite shoes, brown hair ribbons, liberty bodices and the necessity of eating up all one's greens.

'I bet Margot Rose never has to eat cabbage and spinach,' I would mutter rebelliously.

'I don't think that child has ever had a decent meal in her life. I expect they eat baked beans and chips all the time in that house.'

'Sounds alright to me.'

'That's enough, Hilary,' my father would say, lowering his paper and folding it meticulously, always a sign that he was about to make a speech. It was curious, but my parents, who were often and so bitterly divided were presenting a united front in their opposition to my friendship with Margot Rose.

'I don't really think that she is a suitable friend for you,' he continued, 'her father hasn't done a day's work in his life. He claims that he can't because he was wounded in the War. I never heard such nonsense in my life, the man seems perfectly fit to me, especially when he's playing football with his mates and drinking in the pub. It's an insult to the memory of all those brave young men who died.'

My father had lost many of his friends in the War and when he spoke of them his brown eyes looked so raw and helpless that it made me want to cry. He would sometimes speak of boyhood chums with names like Tiger Riley, Biff Baxter and Shortie Grub. It seemed impossible to me that anyone with names like these could have been blown to pieces in the desert or bayoneted by the Japanese in Singapore. They were boys' names, they spoke of midnight feasts, jaunts along the river and schoolboy pranks. They sounded eternally youthful, full of energy and an innocent zest for life. I couldn't believe that they had been wiped out in an instant, knowing only a moment of red, shrieking pain and then oblivion, forever. Neither could my father.

'Damn my eyesight,' he would often say. 'If only I hadn't been as blind as a bat, I would have been able to join the combat troops and fight with them instead of being attached to the Pay Corps.'

My parents, though well meaning, were not astute and they failed to realise that the more they counselled me against Margot Rose, the more determined I became to be with her.

On Thursday afternoons my mother drove into town to do her shopping and I had the house to myself. I would smuggle Margot Rose upstairs and into my parents' bedroom. This was forbidden territory and the enormity of the crime I was committing made me hot and nervous for hours beforehand. It was a large room, facing the sea, and it caught the sun in the afternoons. In the summer there was a clammy undercurrent of stale air which smelt of musty cupboards and heavy winter garments stored away in polythene bags. Thrusting through this came the sharper, more astringent scents of my mother's orange skin food, children's sweaty bodies and hot fabric. My mother was very houseproud and always drew the curtains before she went out to protect the furniture and prevent the carpet from fading. The warm, diluted light, pouring through the thin chintz curtains gave the room an added air of mystery, heightening the feeling of conspiracy between us. We crept across the polished, wooden floorboards clutching each other closely and starting with feigned drama at every creak or unexpected noise.

I thought Margot Rose even more beautiful when she was inside my mother and father's room as though the role of intruder suited her. Stray glimmers of sunlight from the window caught the gold tints in her tangle of auburn hair and the pale light made her creamy skin look faintly luminous. Margot Rose hardly ever had to wear hair ribbons and when she did they were never brown or navy but bright pink or blue and printed all over with little silver stars. How I longed to have hair ribbons like that! She never wore sensible shoes either but white toeless plastic sandals. 'Cheap and Nasty' my mother said, but I adored and coveted them.

All in all I was her willing slave and well she knew it. We would dress up in my mother's nightdresses and petticoats, making veils and headdresses, fastening them around our heads with her stockings. We would transform ourselves into Princesses and Fairy Queens. Margot Rose always seemed to get the best parts.

'I'll be Snow White,' she said, 'and you can be The Seven Dwarfs.'

How I loved those long, secret afternoons we spent together and I hoarded the memories close inside me. Later, alone in my bed I would bring them out and turn them over in my mind, letting them trickle into awareness like a miser running a string of jewels through his fingers. I cherished every moment we spent together, I would shiver with pleasure as I remembered the cool, silky feel of my mother's bedspread, the tingly sensation of Margot Rose's warm breath on the back of my neck, and the salty smell of her skin.

I showed her everything. Crouched together in the small curtained recess between the dressing tables where my mother kept her private papers, I would open the old, cracked white leather handbag and bring out her letters and photographs. Our sticky thighs were pressed tightly together and I was shameless in my need to be accepted. We opened the letters my father had sent in the early days of their marriage when he was posted overseas in the Army and giggled over the gauche sentiments he expressed. Later these would be incorporated into our games and ridiculed. With damp, eager hands we rummaged through the drawers and once I showed Margot Rose an unfamiliar package that had been troubling me for some time.

'Dr. White's Sanitary Towels. Comfortable and highly absorbent. Ideal for those difficult days in the month,' I read out slowly, hesitating over the long words. 'Do you know what these are for Margot Rose? And what does, for those difficult days of the month mean? How can one day be more difficult than any other? At least how would you know it was going to be difficult before it happened?'

'Oh, those things,' she answered. 'We call them Jam Rags. Our Lucinda has to use them now. She says she bleeds like a stuck pig. She says it happens to every girl as they get older.'

'Will it happen to me?'

'Course it will, silly, it happens to everyone. I just told you that.'

I bundled the package hastily back in the drawer and slammed it shut. I turned to her and grabbed her hand.

'Well, I don't want it to happen to me and you. I want us to stay the way we are for ever and ever!'

Sometimes when we tired of my parents' room we would go into my eldest sister's and continue our explorations there. Marlene was nine years older than me and she was a remote figure in my life. She was nearly seventeen and she seemed to spend most of her time gazing out of her window or locked inside her room with her friends. She sighed a great deal and used a lot of words like 'Heavenly' and 'Divine'. She pretended that she could speak Russian and she played the violin, very badly, in front of the mirror, dressed only in a black lace bra and pants.

Margot Rose clutched Marlene's bra against her skinny chest and pirouetted around the room. Her eyelids drooped heavily and her lips pouted. 'Heavenly, darling,' she murmured. 'Quite, quite

Heavenly.' I tottered after her in Marlene's blue suede stiletto heels, scraping raucously on the violin and whispering in what I thought were deeply thrilling tones, 'But Darling, you are Simply Divine. You are just Too, Too Divine.'

On Saturday mornings I would tell my mother that I was going to take my dog, Sam, for a long walk and then I would meet Margot Rose in our secret place beneath the crab-apple tree. The crab-apple tree grew half way up the lane that separated our houses and it was a natural place for us to meet. It was strange countryside around the crab-apple tree, strange and slightly forbidding. Once when Margot Rose had been late I wandered away from the road and found myself in the little wood at the bottom of the garden owned by the man who came from London. There was very little light and the ground was covered with a dark green, foreign-looking plant, that had fleshy leaves and evil, purple-coloured flowers. I was sure it must be poisonous and my skin flinched away from it. There was an inexplicable smell of rusting metal which troubled me. I thought of hatchets and knives and other dangerous implements that might be lying half-buried in the dank soil. It was very quiet at first and then I heard the very faint sound of someone crying. I crept closer until I could see the house. The man from London was sitting on the doorstep, with his head in his hands, sobbing as if his heart would break. I could see the top of his bald head, which was red and flakey with sunburn, and the tears squeezing out between his fingers and dripping onto the hot stones where they sizzled and disappeared as if by magic. I was horrified and disgusted. It was bad enough when my mother cried, but a man! I had never seen a man crying before. An old man at that, and he was crying in broad daylight. It was horrible. Tears were for the darkness, tears were for the young. When I heard Margot Rose calling me from the road I turned and ran, forcing my way through the undergrowth and I didn't stop until I burst out into the hot sunshine and into her arms.

'There now,' she said. 'It's alright, don't fret yourself over him, he won't hurt you. He's just taking on something awful 'cos his wife left him.'

'How do you know?'

'I heard my ma telling her next door, said she didn't blame the poor woman neither, said no self-respecting woman could put up with that miserable old bugger.'

'My mother always makes me leave the room when she's talking to her friends.'

Margot Rose looked at me with a worldly expression far beyond her years.

'Well, your mother, Hilary, your mother's a bit gormless, isn't she? At least that's what my ma says,' she added hurriedly.

One summer, under Margot Rose's instruction, I devoted most of my time teaching Sam to attack wellington boots. I had a particularly horrible pair of boots which my mother made me wear even when the grass was only slightly damp. They had been passed down to me by a whole succession of cousins and I hated them even more than the brown felt hat with bunches of bananas above the ears that I had to wear on Sundays. They were made of a dull, red rubber and around the top was a band of mouldy-looking artificial leopardskin fur. They were the kind of boots much loved by old ladies. Sam was an easy dog to train as he was quite young and it was possible to work him into a frenzy of excitement just by repeating the words 'Canst thou see thine enemies!' in a certain tone of voice. I would run ahead and Sam would chase after me grabbing the leopardskin between his teeth, growling and worrying at it, shaking his head from side to side as if he were a wolf bringing down a sheep.

One afternoon when I was out in the town with my father I saw an old lady walking ahead in an identical pair of boots. Sam was trotting happily beside me and I bent down and whispered in his ear. 'Sam, Sam. Canst thou see thine enemies!' There was a few minutes of wonderful confusion with much snarling from Sam and startled screams from the old lady before my father managed to extricate the hysterical dog from the melée.

'Damn and blast that stupid animal,' he said. 'I just can't think what's got into him lately.'

I felt a mixture of fear and curiosity at the thought of visiting Margot Rose's house. I could always tell what I felt about a house from the way it smelt. As soon as I opened the front door and stepped into the hall of a strange house I could tell whether I liked it or not. Some houses always smelt cold and empty no matter how warm the day and some were full of intimidating smells like boot polish and brasso. In others the smell of stale cooking and cold grease seemed to accumulate just inside the door. I liked to think that I could guess what the family were like from the way their house smelt; that I could tell if they were going to be friendly and relaxed or formal and stiffly polite. This house had a wonderful, intoxicating smell of beer and fried eggs, make-up and clothes steaming in front of the fire. Mrs Tremain was obviously a casual housekeeper and things that would have been hidden away in my house were prominently displayed in hers. Bras and knickers were draped across the backs of chairs and a large bottle of Radcliffe's Worm Syrup stood on the kitchen table. Best of all though was the television. I didn't know anyone else who had a television.

'How can your dad afford to buy a telly if he doesn't have a job?' I asked Margot Rose.

'Well,' she answered, laughing. 'Fell off the back of a lorry, didn't it!'

At first I was shy of Mr Tremain, he seemed so big and meaty compared to my own father, but eventually I found the courage to speak to him. 'Were you really wounded in the War?' I asked. He gave me a long, knowing wink and slowly tapped the side of his nose.

'Well now, my little maid,' he said. 'That would be telling, wouldn't it? Ask no questions and you'll be told no lies.'

Before I met Margot Rose I had been a lonely child seeking consolation in God. I felt I had a special relationship with God because my house was built just below the church and I thought of Him as my next-door neighbour. When I was very young I believed that God lived in the church tower, behind the clock-face. I confused the power of God with the chiming of the clock. 'God is always watching you,' I was told in Sunday school and at night when I woke and it was so quiet that I could hear the hum and whirr of the machinery as the clock prepared to strike I thought that it was God talking to me. The clock would strike the quarters and the halfs, the three quarters and finally the hour and I believed that this was God charting my way through the night, telling me exactly where I was and how long it was till morning, telling me that I was safe, that He was there. I would turn over reassured and go happily back to sleep.

I treated God's garden, the churchyard, as an extension of my own. I would go in through the back gate into the old neglected part of the churchyard where the rusty, iron railings around the graves had collapsed and lay decomposing in great tangles of nettles and goosegrass. Some of the granite tombstones were leaning over at crazy angles, half hidden by the feathery blooms of the elder bushes. Most of the writing on the headstones was so worn that it was impossible to read it and I would clamber up close and trace the letters with my fingers in an effort to find out who was buried there. It was my secret place, and I never told anyone about it, not even Margot Rose. I was always searching for the sailors' graves: I had been told a story once about a shipwreck and I knew that many of the drowned sailors had been buried in the churchyard. Their bodies had never been claimed because no one had been able to find out who they were. 'The Church of St Piran with the graves of the unknown sailors,' I would chant to myself as I thrust my way through the brambles and cow parsley that grew thickly around the graves.

I never did find the sailors' graves but I did find the place where all the babies were buried; it was a remote part of the churchyard, very quiet and still. Here most of the tiny graves were well cared for with fresh flowers and beautiful chips of coloured stone and loving messages inscribed with gold. All of them except one, which lay over in the far corner beneath the wall, a tiny mound of forgotten earth. 'Why had the child's parents left the grave like this?' I wondered. I would spend hours there pondering the mystery and concocting wonderful tales of tragedy to account for it. Perhaps the parents themselves had died from broken hearts or perhaps the entire family had been struck down by some fatal disease. In the end I decided that they just found it too sad to come to visit their baby and so I thought that I would look after the grave for them. For months I kept a jam-jar full of wild flowers and visited the baby regularly. It was the only secret I ever kept from Margot Rose.

I showed her where the Mee Mees lived in the huge stone water tank in the farmyard. I taught her how to catch them and make them a new home in a jam-jar. I took her to my excavations in the dark little shrubbery behind the single-storey wooden house, where poor, mad Mrs McGuire lived. I showed her the curious opaque china bottles and pots I had dug up. 'Mrs McGuire's a witch,' I told her. 'She uses these to mix her potions and poisons in. After you've touched them you have to wash your hands five times with carbolic soap and count backwards from a hundred at the same time. It's the only way to break the spell. Mind now, it has to be carbolic soap or you'll die. I know she's killed a lot of people and she buries them out here; it's only a matter of time before I find the bodies.'

When the tide was right out I led her across the causeway of slippery rocks. I was more agile than she was and I leaped easily from rock to rock ahead of her. When she called to me for help I raced back feeling full of a new confidence; as I took her hand I felt strong and protective towards her. Eventually we reached the end of the causeway and as we peered down through the shifting colours of green and blue light-dazzled water, where the thick brown streamers of seaweed swirled lazily in the current, I showed her the wreckage of the fishing boat. I was proud to share my world with Margot Rose, but I never took her to the baby's grave.

As we grew older our relationship had been changing and our clandestine Thursday afternoons were no longer occupied by children's games. We sat in front of my mother's dressing table practising in earnest with her make up and experimenting with each other's hair. When we had transformed ourselves to our satisfaction we would take all our clothes off and explore each other's bodies with curious fingers. Sometimes we would lie down on the bed and practise snogging and French kissing, tickling and wriggling till our breath came in sharp, hoarse pants. When we bathed together, inching slowly forward into the icy water, our screams contained a new awareness of each other as our bodies responded to the sensation of the sea seeping into the legs of our bathing costumes.

I spent a great deal of time in trying to persuade her to join the church choir. I thought that if only I could have Margot Rose and God together under the same roof then my happiness would be complete. How beautiful she would look in the choir stalls with the light falling through the stained glass windows and haloing her copper-coloured hair. How perfect she would be in the dark purple cassock with the white ruffle setting off her eyes and her pale hand resting on the deeply polished rosewood pew.

'Please Margot Rose,' I begged her. 'Please will you join the choir? Oh, please, please say that you will.'

'Don't be daft. I'm tone deaf and I can't sing a note.'

'But that doesn't matter, I can't sing either. The Vicar doesn't mind whether you can sing or not, he just wants to get enough people to fill up the choir stalls, especially girls, he's very short of girls. He's got a lot of boys, though,' I added slyly knowing this would interest her.

In the end I did persuade Margot Rose to join the choir but it didn't turn out the way I had hoped it would. She refused to take it seriously and mimicked everyone in the choir and the tiny congregation. As we proceeded solemnly up the aisle with the asthmatic old organ wheezing out a hesitant tune, Margot Rose would be convulsed with laughter and her singing would grow progressively louder and more untuneful. 'Be quiet,' I would hiss, digging her hard in the ribs. 'And stop that awful giggling.' She had the most shrill and pervasive giggle that I had ever heard. During the silent prayers she was always peeping between her parted fingers and pulling faces at the Verger. As we recited The Lord's Prayer I could hear her saying 'Our Father who farts in Heaven. Now it's Hallowe'en and he must have ate some beans.' When the Vicar was delivering his sermon she would make loud farting noises just to make the boys laugh.

'Will you shut up,' I said. 'You're being so embarrassing.'

'And you're being so boring. You're being a real pain in the bum.'

One Sunday morning she failed to turn up at all and so did Christopher Curnow, though I didn't notice it at the time. After the service had finished I raced home for Sam and ran all the way to the crab-apple tree, hoping that she would be there waiting for me. As I came round the bend in the lane I saw them. Margot Rose was leaning up against the tree, our tree! And Christopher was bending over her.

'How could she! How could she!' I thought. 'And with Christopher Curnow of all people. Christopher Curnow with his awful pimples and clumsy hands.'

She had smoothed all her lovely hair up into something which she called a French Pleat and she was wearing a turquoise-blue shift dress. 'Tarty', my mother would have called it. The dress was sleeveless and her legs were bare. It was too early in the summer to dress like that and her flesh looked pinched and blue, sort of sad and flabby.

They hadn't seen me and I turned away and crouched down beside Sam. I hugged him to me and pressed his cold nose against my hot cheek. I held him like that for a long moment until he began to whine and struggle to get free. When I looked over to the crab-apple tree, Margot Rose and Christopher had gone.

'Come on, Sam,' I said. 'Let's go home.' ❦

Nancy Brysson Morrison

NO LETTERS, PLEASE

H e sat in his consulting-room, hearing without listening to it the hurried ticking of the small clock on the mantelpiece
behind him eating up the silence. With all the inhibited reserve of
the man who is never interrupted, only now, when the servants were
in bed, did he feel that he had the house to himself, free to go
through the letters lying on top of his desk.

There were shoals of them. He let them run through his fingers
like a pack of cards, only he never played cards. That was
something for which he had never had time. He knew that his
thoughts were only playing with him, while they staved off the

moment he would have to open these squares and oblongs, every one of them.

His reluctance was only natural to read the letters of condolences on his wife's death. This day last week he had not known she was going to die, and as a specialist such prognosis was surely his stock-in-trade. Nobody had known; she herself had received no warning—he had ascertained from Dr. Bolton she had not consulted him for years. His thoughts were numbed solid, as if frozen: the act of thinking cut into them like a snowplough, but they still remained blocks of ice.

If he had known he was going to be faced by this problem, swamped by a sea of condolences, he would certainly have inserted in the intimation 'No letters, please'. That was what some people did, wasn't it? Only 'No letters, please', was usually accompanied by the clause 'No flowers', and she had always loved flowers. He could not have refused them on her behalf.

He simply had not thought about the letters. If he had, he was bound to know he would receive some. But not this avalanche: that was what startled him. He looked down at the varied handwritings: all these people had known her intimately enough to feel they wanted to write to him.

Only one envelope had a black border. He remembered when his father died the scattering of letters his mother had received from far out connections had all been heavily framed in black. Times had changed since then, he thought as he picked up the solitary mourning envelope. No, he contradicted himself, catching sight of his name incorrectly sprawled across it in an illiterate hand, perhaps this class still sent out black-edged notepaper as a token of their respect. He had associated so long with his wife's class that he was inclined to forget he, not the times, had changed in certain things.

He picked up the ivory paper knife lying on his desk and slit it through the envelope in his hand. He must begin some time. From a person called Susan: she had written pages in her clumsy writing that told him her fingers were unaccustomed to a pen. This was more an outpouring than a letter, all about his wife's goodness to the writer not only when she was her mistress but since she married. Never a Christmas or birthday passed but she remembered Susan, some one called Alec, and, of course, the children.

Susan . . . he must have known her, she had lived in this house. His mind tried to work back in an effort to retrieve her from the past, but for the life of him he could not remember her.

And he felt it was vital for him to remember her, as though something, he knew not what except that it was something tremendous, depended on that memory. She wrote how good her mistress had been to her when her mother died—every sentence of the letter, if Susan had gone in for sentences, contained the words 'I'll never forget'. Susan would never forget; and he could not remember one detail about her.

She had called her eldest daughter after his wife. They had no children of their own to be called after her or him, and she had always wanted children. How long ago it was since he had remembered that.

He put Susan's letter to one side. He would have to answer it himself. He could not possibly send to her one of the acknowledgment cards on order. Nor could he allow to pass out of his life the only child to bear her name. He would have to begin and remember Susan from now on, since he could not find her in the past.

It was as though her letter had broken the ice. He did not hesitate opening the next: his name, correct with all his degrees on its envelope, was written with the long 'f's' of foreign script. He noted the signature first—even to him, untutored in such matters, the name rang a bell. Music, like cards, had been another of these things for which he had never had time.

His well known correspondent remembered that the specialist's wife had been his most brilliant pupil; between the lines of his letter it was not difficult to read the frustration of one artist for another whose career had never come to fruition.

He had forgotten all about his wife's piano playing. That must be, he thought, because she never played now, and hadn't for years, although her grand piano still stood, always open, in the drawing room upstairs. Perhaps she had thought piano playing not quite suitable for a specialist's house, when for certain hours each day he used it for consultations. Unless she played it while he was out.

God, he knew nothing about her. This music man, and Susan, knew more about her daily life than he did who had lived with her for well nigh quarter of a century.

He put the letter on top of Susan's—another he would have to answer himself. His hands, with their long, strong, spare fingers, fumbled as he picked up the next envelope, and he peered at the postmark as though his sight were not eagle-clear, as it always was, until he deciphered the name Yetts sealing the stamp.

Yetts! The small country place where he had been born. He saw it again in his mind's eye, the squat grey cottage bordering the patch of village green, and the doctor's house, embosomed in trees, at the other end.

Dr. Elliot had always been good to him: when he, the lad of pairts, came through the university, he knew the doctor had been prepared to have him as a partner; and his practice, in that residential district, was one of the finest in the shire. But everything the lad of pairts did he did with distinction: he had won every honour and prize there was to win. Instead of partnering Dr. Elliot he had married his daughter and specialised. He even looked distinguished now, as though he had been born with a silver not a horn spoon in his mouth.

Whoever could be writing to him from Yetts! He would have thought the last link had been cut years ago. He held the inconspicuous, good envelope in his hand, as though weighing it. But before he opened it, he knew whom it would be from, the only person who would be writing to him from there these days—Kincaid. How long ago it was since he had given him a thought.

Yet how this man had once filled his mind, like an obsession, because both loved the same girl. He could remember the black hatred he had felt for a rival who had everything that he hadn't, everything the world could give him without working or fighting for it. Yet despite that, the girl had chosen not Kincaid but him, the unknown quantity.

How she must have loved him to do that. Now she was no longer there he tried to burrow back into her love for him; to stretch it like a covering over the span that separated now from then. He could read Kincaid's letter with impunity, clothed in the knowledge that he, the reader, was the man who had won, the writer the one who had lost.

Yet no such thoughts filled his mind by the time he had read to the end. It had a curiously humbling effect upon him. Here was one person who knew what he, her husband, must be feeling. The knowledge that Kincaid knew because he had been, perhaps still was in love with her now served to unite him to this man, as though there were kinship between them.

He wrote that he had met her recently when he had been into town. She had not mentioned this visit to her husband, but he thought nothing of that. The musician had said in his letter that he had seen her the last time he was playing with the Scottish Orchestra, and she had not mentioned that to her husband either.

He realised now, when he would never hear her voice again, how little she had mentioned to him. He was, he supposed, a particularly silent man: perhaps that was why she had attracted him so strongly, because she was everything he wasn't, with a quality of gaiety about her. But looking back now, he realised that for years past she must have conformed to his pattern.

He was absorbed by his work and nothing else mattered to him, or had the smallest significance. His reputation was now international. One did not reach where he had reached without a concentration that annihilated, relinquished everything that did not bear on one's subject.

But while he was climbing to the top of his profession, what about her? Had his preoccupation, his silence, had a calcifying effect upon her love for him? He looked down at the sea of letters on his desk. Had she turned to others for the simplest of contacts that he, isolated by himself, had denied her?

You could look at a woman, sit at the same table with her, every day of your life, and not see her. That was what he had done. He had taken her as much for granted in his life as he took a piece of furniture in a room he used every day.

But she would understand: she had always understood. Understood what? That he loved her, although he had taken her for granted, that she was the background to his life, as necessary to him as the air he breathed. Because she knew him as no one else knew him, she must have known what he felt for her, what he would feel if she were taken from him. If only he could be sure that she knew that—

He must speak of her to some one, some one who had known her. Only thus could he feel in touch with her as he had been once upon a time. Kincaid—he was the one person he could contact. In some unexplained way he felt Kincaid came into this, because he could remember her, himself, the other fellow when they had all been young.

As he waited while the call was put through he realised how the intervening years had evened things out between him and the man he was now telephoning. No longer did he smart under a sense of inferiority. He and his one-time rival were equals now. Indeed, he was more than equal to him, he was his better—because she had chosen to be his wife.

Kincaid did not sound surprised to hear who was ringing him at that hour, but if he had been he would not have revealed it. There were some things he would never need to learn, because they were part and parcel of him. The specialist heard his own voice stumble, he who was customarily incisive and to the point.

'Your letter . . . it was good of you to write as you did . . . I telephoned to say to you what I could not write.' The sigh that escaped him reached the other prolonged and exaggerated. 'I cannot tell you what I feel about what happened, but I know you understand.' Despite his faltering, he found he could speak to this disembodied voice as he could never have spoken to him in person. He began to feel disembodied himself. 'It all happened within a matter of hours, you see.'

'Always those you love are young to die.'

He understood, this man at the other end, understood as no one else could.

'I did not know you had seen her so recently.'

So anxious was he to reach what he was leading up to that he was unaware of the infinitesimal pause before the other replied.

'No? She did not mention it to you then?'

'No, but of course she wouldn't. I've always been so busy that I'm afraid I got out of the way of listening to the come and go of daily life. But you do think that she knew what I felt for her, don't you? That although perhaps I gave no sign it didn't mean that I didn't love her? If only I could be sure of that, what a difference it would make to me. This last time you saw her, for instance, did she—what I mean is—well, did she let fall anything which made you know whether she were happy or unhappy?'

Eternity yawned for him in a chasm of a pause as the other remembered back.

'As a matter of fact, her last words to me were—'

He had the feeling that Kincaid had the strongest reluctance to tell him.

'Yes?' he asked desperately. 'What did she say to you?'

'There is only one man in my life. There will always only be one man.'

His relief was such that only then did he realise how much had hung on this man's reply.

'She said that of me?' His grip tightened on the receiver as he waited for the joy of hearing it repeated.

But Kincaid's voice sounded remote, almost formal, as he replied, 'These were her very words.'

No wonder he had been reluctant to tell him what the woman he loved had said of him, her husband. Naturally he could not guess what her words meant to the man at the other end—only he knew that, because only he could feel as he felt now.

When he had rung off he returned to his desk. Although his unfrozen feelings hurt him with their pain, pain was better than that deadening numbness. You had to be alive to feel.

He sat far into the night reading the letters on his desk, piling each one he read on top of Susan's. As he must answer hers by hand so would he have to answer every single one. They were no longer letters of condolences. They were life-lines to his love. ❦

ACKNOWLEDGEMENTS

For permission to reprint copyright material the publishers gratefully acknowledge the following:

Susan Chaney: 'First Love' from *Original Prints* II (Polygon, 1990).

Deirdre Chapman: 'The New Place' from *The Grafton Book of Scottish Short Stories* (1985) by permission of Harper Collins.

Ian Hamilton Finlay: 'A Broken Engagement' by permission of the author.

George Friel: 'An Angel in his House' first published in *World Review* (1952), also in *A Friend of Humanity and Other Stories* (Polygon, 1992).

Janice Galloway: 'where you find it' by permission of the author and A.P. Watt Ltd.

Neil M. Gunn: 'The Old Man' by permission of Faber and Faber Limited.

Patricia Hannah: 'Tintin in Edinburgh' by permission of the author.

James Kelman: 'Ten Guitars' from *Not Not While the Giro* (Polygon, 1985).

A.L. Kennedy: 'Tea and Biscuits' from *Original Prints III* (Polygon, 1989).

Gordon Legge: 'I Never Thought it would be You' from *In Between Talking About the Football* (Polygon, 1991).

Eric Linklater: 'Sealskin Trousers' from *Penguin Book of Scottish Short Stories* (Penguin, 1983).

George Mackay Brown: 'Andrina' from *Andrina and Other Stories* (Chatto and Windus/The Hogarth Press, 1983) by permission of Chatto and Windus.

Bernard MacLaverty: 'A Pornographer Woos' from *Secrets* (Blackstaff Press).

Susie Maguire: 'The Day I Met Sean Connery' by permission of the author.

Duncan McLean: 'Come Go With Me' from *Cutting Edge*, by permission of the author.

James Meek: 'Survival and the Knee' from *Last Orders* (Polygon, 1992).

Naomi Mitchison: 'On an Island' from *Classic Scottish Short Stories* (OUP, 1963).

Nancy Brysson Morrison: 'No Letters, Please' from *Casual Columns: The Glasgow Herald Miscellany* by permission of George Outram & Co. Ltd.

James Robertson: 'What Love Is' from *The Ragged Man's Complaint* (1993) by permission of b&w ltd.

Peter D. Robinson: 'The Wabe' from *And Thus Will I Freely Sing* (Polygon, 1989) by permission of the author.

Dilys Rose: 'All the Little Loved Ones' from *Red Tides* (Secker and Warburg, 1992).

Ali Smith: 'The World with Love' from *Free Love* (Virago, 1995).

Iain Crichton Smith: 'Christmas Day' from Selected Stories (Carcanet).

Muriel Spark: 'A Member of the Family' from *Voices at Play* (Macmillan, 1961).

Kay West: 'The Single Bed Years' from *The Crazy Jig* (Polygon, 1992).